A FORCED PROXIMITY HOLIDAY ROMANCE

Two

of a

Kind

ASHLEY PINES   EDEN EMORY

Content Notes

This is a work of fiction. Names, characters, business, events and incidents are the products of the author's imagination. Any resemblance to actual persons, living or dead, or actual events is purely coincidental. Before moving forward, please note that the themes in this book can be dark and trigger some people.

Tropes/Tags: Forced Proximity, Christmas Romance, New York City Ball Drop, Longing, Miscommunication

Content Warnings: Grief, passing away of a loved one (off page), cancer(off page), O denial, feelings of abandonment, explicit sex .

If you need help, please reach out to the resources below.

Content Notes

National Domestic Violence Hotline

1-800-799-7233

https://www.thehotline.org/

Also by Ashley Pines

Queer romance that kills

Devil's Playground

Hide N' Seek

Rat Race

Novellas

Two of a Kind: A forced proximity sapphic holiday romance

Bex Deveau

Monstrously Romantic Queer Polyam

Underworld University

Deal With the Devil

The Devil I Know

Neon Immortals

Bite Marks (Pre-Order!)

Claws + Cappuccinos

Love Potions + Paperwork

Also by Eden Emory

Two of a Kind

Club Pétale World:

The Ties that Bind Us

Don't Stop Me

Don't Leave Me

Don't Forget Me (2023)

Elle Mae (Paranormal)

Short and Smutty:

The Sweetest Sacrifice: An Erotic Demon Romance

Nevermore: A Deal with a Demon

Blood Bound Duology:

Contract Bound: A Lesbian Vampire Romance

Lost Clause (2023)

Winterfell Academy Series:

The Price of Silence: Winterfell Academy Book 1

The Price of Silence: Winterfell Academy Book 2

The Price of Silence: Winterfell Academy Book 3

The Price of Silence: Winterfell Academy Book 4

The Price of Silence: Winterfell Academy Book 5

Other World Series:

An Imposter in Warriors Clothing

A Coward In A Kings Crown

For those wishing for an angsty sapphic holiday romance, this is for you

A FORCED PROXIMITY HOLIDAY ROMANCE

Two
of a
kind

ASHLEY PINES   EDEN EMORY

Chapter 1

Hazel

Christmas used to be my favorite holiday.

I loved the way that the snow blanketed the city, turning the hustle and bustle of New York into something almost quaint and homey. The strings of lights dotting the trees and fire escapes. The familiar to the point of irritation carols on the radio, especially Michael and Mariah's covers of the classics. The little frosted shortbread cookies from the bodega down the street, best served with hot chocolate with a dash of cinnamon—but that was B.C.D., *before Chris died.*

Now, Mariah crooning over the radio left me feeling sick with memories of the last time the snow stuck to the tree tops and the tiny front yard of my brownstone. The day I got the news that fucked up every one of my best-laid plans and destroyed the most important relationship in my life.

Northern Vermont passed the window in a blur of evergreen and white as we sailed down the winding, five-mile-long driveway to the Williams' cabin. Chris' family had been kind enough to give me the keys so that we could keep our tradition of spending Christmas at Stargazer's Lake.

Like the name suggested, it was a lake known for the best views of the stars in the entire continental United States—or at least that's what their travel brochure advertised.

For miles it was nothing but cabins nestled into the thick woods with *just* enough space around each of them to make it feel like you were truly secluded. And, for the most part, it was. We could stay here for weeks and never run into anyone else. Though, just in case, there was a gas station turned supermarket for the locals five miles before the winding hill that led you to the lake. It didn't have much besides chips, almost expired milk, and stale bread, but it would do for whatever unlucky soul ran out of food during their trip.

A sort of chill ran through me, despite the warm air coming from the SUV's vents.

It was the first time in three years that I wasn't snuggled up to Chris' side as he drove, manning the playlist and feeding him bits of homemade gingerbread cookies. Instead, Lexie had offered her SUV and its heated seats for the five-hour drive north, a tin of cookies rattling in my lap with every bump. We listened to the radio, a mix of pop hits interspersed with Christmas favorites and warnings of an impending snowstorm.

The rest of the Latin 101 Study Group—the name of our ancient group chat despite the fact that we'd all long since graduated—would meet us by the end of the afternoon.

Well, everyone except Chris.

I swallowed hard and leaned my cheek against the cold window.

If I'd known what was going to happen, I would've taken a thousand more photos. Now all I was left with was the weight of his absence. It didn't matter if I was on the subway or surrounded by the people who loved me—at the end of it all none of them could replace what I'd lost.

The image of a familiar flash of dirty blonde hair and a

frown passed through my mind and caused my chest to constrict, but I pushed away the thoughts before I could linger on why thinking of *her* caused me to react that way.

"Are you even listening?" Lexie asked gently, her manicured hand sliding from the wheel to touch my arm where I'd rested it on the center console.

"Sorry, lost in the past," I muttered, stretching my legs the best I could in the confined space. "Being back here—"

"Brings up a lot of memories. Yeah, I figured." Another squeeze of fingers against my arm warned me we were quickly heading into sympathy territory.

"Please, not again with the pity party. I'm *fine*, Lexie," I groaned.

It'd been like this for eleven months.

I pretend to be fine—sometimes even *feel* fine—and my friends would treat me like I'm made of glass or likely to burst into tears at any second. They treated me like an entirely different person. Like I wasn't Hazel, the happy go lucky life of the party. To them I was *broken*.

Well, the ones that cared enough to call at least.

I hadn't heard anything from my so-called best friend since Chris' funeral last December.

For fuck sake, I'd stopped crying about it in March! I wasn't some tragic almost-widow. I was so over it I'd even downloaded Tinder—Sure, I'd never made a profile, but it was progress!

That wasn't what this trip was about anyway. We were supposed to be celebrating! Enjoying our time together!

All of us, for the first time since the funeral.

Even *Quinn*, who despite watching all of my Instagram stories wouldn't return my calls or texts.

I stifled a sigh.

No matter how hard I tried to keep her out of my mind, she always found a way in.

"It's kind of crazy," Lexie muttered, fiddling with the temperature knobs. "Being up here without him."

"Yeah," I said noncommittally.

It wasn't that I didn't want to talk about him—of course we would—but I wasn't going to cry on this trip.

I was sick and tired of grieving. I'd done my fair share of it. I didn't want his death to be the thing that defined me any more. I was ready to move on. And desperate for a week full of snowball fights, hot chocolate, and overly posed Instagram updates. I'd even left my laptop at home so I wouldn't be able to work—save for a few fun stories or TikToks.

A real vacation. Not the brand paid trips and 'holidays' I'd taken as often as possible. Drowning myself in work had been an excellent way to distract myself, at least for a while. Now I was burnt-out on top of missing Chris and Quinn.

Alex honked the horn of his Jeep behind us, swerving back and forth on the road and kicking up snow behind his tires.

Despite living in New York with us, Alex and Matt had to bring their own car since Lexie and I brought enough luggage for the two of us as everyone else would combined. But hey, that was the life of a blogger and her designer bestie. We'd do some quick promo shots of her winter line while we were up here and I'd get some new—100% sustainable and equitably made—clothes to wear as payment.

"Those idiots are going to crash," Lexie scoffed, rolling down her window and sticking her arm out with her middle finger up. Behind us, the constant swerving ceased amid a barrage of honking as we turned and pulled up in front of a massive, two-story cabin made entirely of sealed wood logs.

My breath caught in my throat like it had ever since I'd first laid eyes on the two-story hideaway, a sense of calm washing over me like a balm to my anxious heart. I'd been so *jealous* the first time Chris brought me up here. There was no way that my

Mom—feeding me and my two brothers by herself on a nurse's salary—could've afforded to even rent a place like this.

The trees surrounding us acted like a barrier to the outside world. Fluffy white snow stuck to every surface piled so high— even though I knew I would instantly regret it—all I could imagine was diving straight into it.

Thank God the Williams had someone plow the drive during the winters. There's no way Lexie's sporty SUV would have made it through the waist high drifts. Beyond the cabin you could see the frozen surface of the lake, a mass of blank space circled by pine trees. The next nearest cabin was over a quarter a mile away, which meant we were perfectly, wonderfully *alone*.

As much as I hated life without Chris, there was something to be said about being truly alone. To be away from the world and not having to worry about life. Just another reason why I'd fallen so in love with this place.

While we were here, it was like the real world didn't exist. No more brand deals, deadlines or engagement statistics. Here, I could do whatever I wanted. *Be* whatever I wanted. And as someone who'd made a career out of being visible 24/7, entertaining 24/7—being alone and *myself* was more invaluable than a front-row seat to Girl In Red.

I hopped out of the car, leaving the cookies on the seat and stopping to look up at the cabin's angular windows. Its triple peaked roof cut into the gray sky like the spires of a castle, housing the bedrooms that would act as ours for the next week. The wrap-around porch was covered in a light dusting of sticky snow, perfect for—

An orb of tightly packed powder hit the back of my olive green jacket, exploding on impact and I squealed, diving to the side and packing up a handful in my bare hands.

Alex darted past me and up the stairs, trying to close the

door before I could return fire. But he was slow from too many long nights in his swanky uptown office full of free snacks, and my snowball made its mark, exploding along the back of his head.

"Oh, you are *DONE!*" Alex shouted, racing back down the steps towards me and Lexie, who'd already taken up a fistful of snow.

"Run!" she shrieked, darting behind the SUV as snow hit the window where she was just standing.

Matt pushed his glasses up his nose, lobbing another icy projectile my way; I ducked and made a break for cover behind the car, realizing my mistake much too late.

"We have no ammo!" I shouted to Lexie.

She pulled a strand of her severe blonde bob from where it had gotten stuck in her lip gloss and grinned. "We need to make a break for the trees!"

"Come out, come out, wherever you are!" Alex shouted, his boots loud on the pavement.

Lexie giggled, her blue eyes shining. "Okay, three…"

"Two…" I returned, my muscles tense and ready to run.

"One!" Lexie shouted, jumping up and running towards the trees on the side of the drive.

Alex grabbed her around the waist, hoisting her off the ground and tossing her into a snowdrift with a maniacal laugh I hadn't heard in way too long.

I moved to go the other way but it was too late. Matt grabbed me and slung me over his shoulder with a grunt of effort, his thick-rimmed glasses sliding down his nose.

"Not so fast, Hazel. You have a date with a snowdrift."

"No!" I wailed, struggling in his grip. For a lawyer Matt was shockingly buff.

He held my face just above the icy powder. "Sorry gorgeous, you started it."

Chapter 2

Quinn

I was not a fan of get-togethers.

Especially when it came to holing up in a cabin in the middle of nowhere where the snow was threatening to bury us alive. Double especially not when I would have to leave my nice, toasty apartment but I would have to *live* with five other people for God knows how long.

Don't get me wrong, I loved my friends. They were all very nice people who'd been with me since my awkward college years. The people who had seen me fail at every attempt to be a responsible adult and helped me laugh it off as I found out what I was passionate about.

They tried to support me when I was a bartender, no matter how snappy I had gotten with the customers. Or cheered me on when I had joined a random indie band playing the drums, even though I was horrible. And then when I sold myself to a boring old customer service job taking calls from technologically inept people, they still had nothing bad to say.

They saw that I was trying hard, and to them, that was all that mattered.

Like Max, who'd graciously volunteered to drive me up the snow-covered mountain in her beat up Honda. A part of me knew that she'd only asked me to come with her because she was afraid that if she didn't, I wouldn't come at all. But when I opened the passenger side door to see the wrinkliest, smelliest puppy I had met in my entire life, I knew why she'd insisted on driving up separately from everyone else.

He was now curled up in my lap, snoring lightly without a care in the world as he napped. Even though his hair was short there would no doubt be an accumulation of it left on my sweats and hoodie, leaving them unwearable for the rest of the trip.

Perfect.

To add onto my irritation, Max was in the driver's seat singing at the top of her lungs to an upbeat song I swear I'd only heard on beat up dance machines at the back of the arcade we used to frequent. At least then there were beers and pizza.

Chris held the high score on that stupid machine up until three weeks ago. I'd gone to visit it a few times since he'd died. Usually when I wanted to talk to him. Or to Hazel.

It was stupid, but it made me feel like he was still here.

I cast a glance at the redhead, unable to hold in my grimace. She hunched over the steering wheel with her eyes focused on the road in front of us. She wore a green hoodie with a white vest, and jeans. Her shoulder length hair in stark contrast to the blurry whiteness of the snow we passed. Even though we'd cranked up the heat in her car, her light freckled skin was spotted with red from the cold. She met my eye with a smile. If I'd been less nervous, I might not have noticed how her hands gripped the steering wheel with a force that turned her knuckles white. Or how her smile fell when she realized she'd been looking at me for way too long.

Max turned down the music with a shaky hand.

"Lighten up, Quinn," she said with a smile. "We're almost there."

"If your shitty car doesn't give up on us first," I said with a huff, shifting so I could pull my phone out of my pocket. Service was pretty spotty on the way up but there was still enough that I could pull up Instagram. At least it would be something to focus on so I wouldn't go crazy hoping that the car would make it up the hill.

"Hey! She's not shitty," Max said with a pout, running her hand lovingly on the dash. "She's been with me since our Latin days, she deserves respect."

"She deserves to be put down," I grumbled, returning my focus to my phone.

It was almost like muscle memory, the way my fingers hit the explore tab and went to the search bar. Hazel's profile was waiting in the history, after I'd searched it so many times before to this.

Hazel—my ex and one of our friends and the entire reason we were going up to the cabin. Well... Hazel had always been more than *just* an ex or *just* a friend. She had been the first and last of many. A person I never thought I would ever have loved as much as I did. But, like all things, that passed. At least that was what I would have hoped to believe. My frown deepened when I caught the date on her profile with the little dove emoji next to it. Her fiancé, Chris, and another one of our friends had sadly passed away from colon cancer just last year.

I tried not to think of Chris too much. Both before and after his death. We were close friends, sometimes I would think even as close as Hazel and I were, but it was kinda hard to keep a close relationship with him when I was always stuck as their third wheel.

I enjoyed being around them. Both of them were such happy, carefree people that it was hard *not* to want to be around them constantly. No matter where it was or what we were doing, as long as they were around, we could be happy.

He was the most selfless person I had ever met—besides Max, my best friend. Or at least, she was now that Hazel and I were nothing more than ghosts of each other's past.

I don't know what drew me to him in the first place. He was charismatic. Charming. Had a way with people that would make them say yes to even the craziest of things.

And he had *Hazel.*

Those two were a match made in heaven; I couldn't even be mad when they were together. It didn't matter what we had between us, or the lack thereof. Everything else seemed to fall away until it was just them against the world.

I loved both of them too much to wish them anything but happiness.

Maybe that was another gift of Chris', it was impossible to be mad at him for anything he did. Even before the cancer.

We made a tradition of going up to his family's cabin every year for winter break back in college. I wasn't huge on the holiday, but something about the peace of Stargazer's Lake and the smell of homemade gingerbread brought warmth to my chest. Plus, we'd get drunk off our asses and have the time of our lives. It was a great way to forget about the responsibilities that were waiting for us at home.

Even though I hated any type of crowd or party, I found myself waiting every year for the time that we would spend at the cabin.

Hazel's Instagram was filled with pictures of her in the most magnificent places. Like Chris, she had this aura about her that just drew people in. I remember how I used to tease her about how online she was, back when careers in such a space were nonexistent, but she kept up with it and proved me wrong.

It was hard not to be proud of her.

I'd seen her newest picture over a hundred times now but I still clicked on it. A posed image of her on a mountain pass, snow piled around her like fluffy white clouds. She was dressed in a huge puffy jacket that seemed to swallow her small frame whole, smiling at the camera so hard her nose scrunched and her eyes were barely visible.

A picture that screamed *happiness*, but if you knew her well enough you may notice how her skin had lost its color. How her cheeks had sunken in. The lack of light in her eyes.

I knew that in the unedited photo there would be dark circles under her eyes. I'd seen them in the temporary stories that she posted to her profile.

I watched every single one of them. Liked every photo. But every time her name flashed across my screen ... I couldn't bring myself to pick up.

I wouldn't dare.

The guilt was already too much to bear. It ate my insides. Kept me up in the middle of the night pacing my studio. I'd seen the sunrise so many times in the last eleven months it was a wonder I didn't have circles to match Hazel's.

"You know there's going to be an update soon," Max said conversationally. "She'll get a notification every time you look at her profile."

My entire body flushed and my head snapped to her. There was a devilish smirk spreading across her freckled face that spelled '*caught you*'.

"Not funny, *Maxine*," I hissed. The blood that rushed to my cheeks coupled with the heat of the AC blasting my face was unbearable now. "If you keep that up, I'll tell *the entire* group that you said the only present you wanted for Christmas was to be in between not one but *two* of our—"

Her mouth fell open and she let out a strangled noise of horror between a gasp and a scream, cutting off my threat.

"You *wouldn't!*" she hissed. "I'm just saying that maybe you should spend less time stalking her socials and more time *actually* talking to her."

I let out a loud groan, causing the dog to stir in my lap. He stretched, his mouth emitting a high pitched yawn that made me wince. But when his big, dark eyes met mine, I couldn't help but give in and scratch between his ears.

He went back to sleep in mere seconds, content to let me feed him attention.

"I *can't,* Max," I said in an exasperated tone, ripping my beanie off and running my hand through my short blonde hair. "You all may be able to get over everything that happened to Chris. What he asked of us... but I can't. Not when I–"

I cut myself off before the emotions became too much.

This was *exactly* why I was thinking of skipping the trip altogether. As much as I wanted to honor Chris's memory and as much as I wanted to see Hazel ... I was toeing a dangerous fucking line.

"I said *talk to her.* You know, like normal friends?" The irritation in her tone was obvious. "Not confess your *undying love.*"

"Don't project onto me," I mumbled lamely.

She had a point and she knew it. As much as it annoyed me, Max had been a really good friend to me since Chris died. I didn't just lose him last year, I'd lost Hazel too.

Though, if I was honest, the second part was my fault—but it was easier to blame Chris.

My eyes shifted to the Stargazer's Lake welcome sign, wooden and painted with cheery little evergreens. It wouldn't be long before we'd be driving down that winding driveway and come face to face with the rest of the group for the first time since the funeral.

And *Hazel*.

I tried to steel myself but it was fruitless with the way my heart was pounding in my chest, my anxiety at an all time high as sweat broke out across my skin.

Max clicked her tongue as we turned the corner. The cabin was in sight now—and so were the cars parked outside. If I squinted I could make out the figures of our friends sitting on the porch, something in their hands.

As we got closer I could make out the mugs that they held. They were laughing and smiling, even Hazel who sat on the bench against the wall of the house. There was a blanket on her shoulders and her cheeks and nose were pink from the cold. It reminded me of the last time we were here.

Reminded me of the time we laid in the snow, watching the stars above as the rest of the house slept. She had been restless like she always was when confined in a small place for too long. We reminisced about the past and tried to pick out totally made up constellations from the clear night sky.

It was one of the last times I saw her truly happy.

I couldn't stop staring at *her* as we came to a stop behind the cars. She looked better than she did at the funeral, but everything that I'd thought while looking at her photos was true.

She'd lost weight and even though she was smiling and laughing with our friends, there was a tenseness to her. The carefree Hazel I'd come to know was buried under eleven months of loneliness.

When everyone's gaze snapped to us I was forced to pull my eyes from her. I looked towards Max who was already giving me a knowing look.

"*Projecting*, huh?" she asked under her breath, turning off the engine.

I shook my head, climbing out of the car with the pup secured in my arms. Immediately the attention was on me and the dog as Max yelled for the others to come look.

"—He's so precious!"

I met our friends with a forced smile. Made the pleasant, polite small talk that was expected of me. But as soon as Hazel made her way over to us, my breath was knocked out of my chest.

Her dark hair fell around her in waves, reaching the middle of her ribs. She pushed a lock behind her ear as our eyes met, giving me a look at her flushed skin. Her green eyes flickered from me to the puppy and she pushed off her steaming mug of what I assumed was hot cocoa to the closest willing hands, which happened to belong to Alex, so that she could grab him from me.

Her rich floral scent hit me in a wave, sending me back to the days that we'd spend cuddled in my dorm room, talking about everything and anything. Unlike then, when her hands brushed across my front, they didn't linger. Accidental instead of full of intent. Her warmth sinking into my skin then *gone* before I could enjoy it.

With a forced smile, she turned and took the attention of our friends with a giggle. "Look at the little baby!"

Forgetting completely about me.

If guilt wasn't strangling me, I may have been hurt, but instead I followed our friends inside the cabin—pretending to be the friend she needed. Just another one of Chris' old buddies.

Regardless of what the lingering eyes of our friends had said about the interaction that was all we were.

Hazel was grieving.
And I was her friend.

Chapter 3

Hazel

I wasn't in the habit of lying to myself.

Not about how I was feeling.

Not about how I felt about others.

Not even about the crushing weight of the grief I carried around like a trendy, designer handbag.

But as I turned away from Quinn and back to our friends, I could hardly keep the smile from slipping right off my face. She looked the same as always—all short, dirty blonde hair and tattoos that peeked out of the collar of her hoodie. Familiar, but like a stranger was standing in her skin.

And it *hurt* to see her. More than I'd thought. I'd tried to prepare myself—told myself over and over that it wouldn't be a big deal—but now that it was here, now that *she* was here ... I started to understand just how uncomfortable this holiday would be.

At least we weren't sharing a room.

The ease of our relationship had evaporated in a year of declined calls and ignored text messages. I'd be so desperate over the summer I'd even shown up to her apartment, banged on her door, and waited for an hour to see if she'd let me in. And *nothing*.

She'd turned her back on me and so *easily*. And after years of her being the only one I could rely on, the betrayal cut deep.

I guess best friends weren't forever.

For the most part, I was keeping it together. But in that brief look we'd shared, it was like I was bleeding out all over the snow. The wounds of the last year are as fresh as if we were back at Chris' funeral, stealing a moment of ecstasy in the vicar's broom closet.

I *needed* her this last year. She knew that. She'd been there to see it all—to watch Chris decline. When he got better and looked like he was going to defy the odds. And when that progress slipped through my fingers like sand and I could do nothing but sob into her stupid zip up hoodie with the holey elbow. But even after all that, she'd left me out to dry.

Like I was nothing. Like *we* were nothing.

"Isn't he sweet?" I cooed in a falsely cheerful voice, ever the center of attention.

Before Lexie picked me up I'd practiced smiling in the mirror for hours. Mostly for my friends, to show them that I was not as breakable as they thought I was, but this smile felt like it was for me. To tell myself that as long as I was here, I would be happy. Those muscles didn't fail me now as I shuffled the pug in my arms where I stood on the soft, high pile rug, my boots kicked off near the door.

Matt made grabby hands for the bundle of wiggly cuteness and I obliged instantly, handing the puppy over to his baby talk. "Aren't you the cutie-wootiest? A whittle baby puggy-wuggy!"

Alex and Max shared a long hug in greeting, her cheeks tinged pink when they separated. Then she had her arms wrapped around me, squeezing the air from my lungs.

"I love your hair like this, you look all dark and mysterious." She grinned and I laughed, giving her a tight squeeze back.

"I wasn't feeling very blonde anymore."

A half lie, but they didn't need to know what I had to do in order to keep the thoughts of Chris out of my mind while cooped up in our empty townhouse. It was either that or travel and sponsorships had been a little dry ever since I had a lapse in my posting schedule after his death.

Lexie bounded up behind us, wrapping us both into what was quickly becoming a group hug with me at its center. It was sort of a relief, it meant I didn't have to think about how the fuck I was supposed to make my hello with Quinn less awkward.

It wasn't even supposed to be my problem! I'd called, texted, and everything else I could think of. *She* froze me out, not the other way around.

And yet I was the one who felt I had stones in my stomach.

How *pathetic*.

"A little space, guys?" I asked hopefully, only to be squeezed harder by two sets of arms.

"Get in here Alex!" Lexie shouted and the brunette obliged, albeit half-heartedly, wrapping his arms around the three of us awkwardly.

"Go team?" he asked in his gravelly voice, his hand finding the top of my head through the mess of bodies for a quick pat.

"Let's make dinner!" called Matt. "What's this little angel's name, by the way?"

"Milo," Quinn said, her voice turning my insides into goo— the same texture as a perfectly melted marshmallow. Overly sweet and smoky and—

Fuck. Of course. *Of course.* I couldn't help but completely dissolve the second I saw her.

I pretended to enjoy the group hug for a few moments more, just long enough to swallow my tears.

Despite how angry at her I was, how hurt I felt—I *missed* Quinn this last year. Missed her enough that I'd kept calling. Kept texting. Checked my story watches obsessively to see if she was thinking about me ... or if her finger slipped and she'd watched accidentally.

The group released me. Max and Alex bounding after Matt and Milo into the kitchen with an uptick of chatter. Lexie following close behind.

I swallowed hard as Quinn's footsteps drew closer over the floorboards. I'd been waiting for this moment since the last time we parted, and now that it was here I would've given anything to delay it another few minutes. Or hours. However long it would take me to figure out how to do this—be friends again— without making a total fool of myself.

"Hi."

I turned, meeting her blue eyes, the color of the aqua-marines in the bracelet I still wore everyday. The bracelet she bought me as a graduation present. "Hi."

"How're you?"

"Fine." I fought the urge to draw my lip between my teeth.

Didn't I know how to say more than one word at a time? Hadn't I been waiting for this exact moment?

Still, no matter how many times I had practiced what I was going to say, all the words died on my tongue and I was left a floundering mess.

It didn't help that her gaze never wavered from mine.

"You?"

"Fine," Quinn murmured, her voice like a balm to the part of my heart that'd been hurting since I said goodbye to my fiancé and my best friend in the same day. I'd been wrong these last few months, there wasn't a *Chris* sized hole in my life, there was a *Chris* and *Quinn* shaped hole.

"I'm..." I started and trailed off, hooking my thumb towards the kitchen where the sound of sizzling and the smell of bacon drifted towards us.

"Yeah."

I turned and all but ran for the kitchen, slipping a little in my woolen socks on the hardwood. I inserted myself easily into the fray with our friends, taking a round of drink orders and making quick work of beers and cups of tea.

Anything to keep my hands busy. And to keep me from staring at Quinn. Or crying.

Or thinking about Chris.

Tomorrow, a few of us would need to go into town and pick up groceries and drinks for the rest of the week since we'd only brought enough liquor to last us the night. A fact highlighted by the half full bottle of whiskey I'd tucked into the snowbank just outside the glass patio door that led to the back porch—after carefully avoiding having to look straight at Quinn, who sat herself at the kitchen island, of course.

Glen Breton, it'd been Chris' favorite. I had to order it from this tiny distillery in butt-fuck nowhere Nova Scotia, Canada.

I collected my glass as my friends threw together a quick breakfast-for-dinner situation. Plates of eggs and bacon and toast appearing on the counter between conversations about work and travel and our lack of boyfriends—or girlfriends, in the case of Quinn, Alex, and Matt.

One thing about the Williams'—they *hated* camping. Which meant the 'cabin' was fitted with the amenities us city folk were accustomed to. It'd cost them a fortune and a half to run power and water all the way out here, but damn did it ever improve our holidays.

Even for such a simple meal, I had used all the eggs and

bacon they had loaded into the fridge. I prayed that they had extra in the car and we wouldn't be stuck with cans of soups and tuna that had been stowed away in the cabinet.

The open concept living and dining area opened up to a massive back patio that overlooked the lake. A wood stove and comfortable, buttery leather sectional the highlight of the space. Tucked into the side of the wall with massive floor to ceiling windows were a pair of bunk beds, a bathroom just beyond them rounding out the main floor.

We ate quickly at the island, swapping stories about the last year and passing the puppy nibbles of toast and bacon when we thought the others weren't looking.

Alex's company had been nominated for some huge award in the tech space.

Matt had helped with the contracts for the latest batch of recruits into the NBA.

Lexie's collection of sustainable evening wear was picked up by Harrods.

Max was promoted to the manager of the shelter she worked at.

Mostly, I looked resolutely at anyone but Quinn. She'd made herself perfectly fucking clear by ignoring my calls and messages. Being stuck together for a week wouldn't change that fact.

She didn't want to talk to me.

After the dinner dishes had been cleared, Matt—with some help from Alex—hauled the massive nine foot tree out of the storage closet, Max trailing after them with a few boxes of ornaments. It was a ridiculous thing, but part of the tradition was decking this palace out in full holiday garb.

"Dibs on turning it on!" shouted Lexie excitedly from beside me on the couch. We sipped our whiskey as the others put the tree together. Matt did most of the heavy lifting, but

Alex was a wizard at fluffing the branches and making the whole thing look new again, no matter how many times we tossed the old thing back into the storage closet hungover.

Lexie nudged me with her foot. "So..." she mock whispered.

"Don't," I grumbled under my breath, sucking back at least a finger of the whiskey in one go.

Quinn had settled into the lone armchair in the room, her knee bouncing as she watched Max and the guys with Milo on her lap. The fact that she had settled with the pup, even though she looked at it with such obvious distaste, caused warmth to bloom in my chest. She had never been a person that did well around ... *messy* things, including animals. So to see that she was still letting the puppy shed and slobber all over her said something about her ability to change.

I hopped off the sofa before Lexie could reply, riffling through the open box of ornaments to find some of my favorites. Part of our tradition was that every year we brought a new ornament based on something that'd happened, which meant that there were a whole fuck ton of memories wrapped in scraps of leftover tissue paper.

Memories, that despite my pledge not to cry during this trip, quickly had my eyes filling with tears. I took a deep breath, willing the tightness in my throat to subside as I pulled out a glittering, golden 'C' with red ribbon from the box.

It was a silly thing, really. A tradition that wasn't ever supposed to be a tradition. Started when Chris' Mom, Joanne, had bought all of us one of these golden letters for the tree the first year we'd come to the cabin together.

I dug the rest of the letters out of the box, blinking rapidly to dispel the tears and pasting an Instagram ready smile onto my face. "Max, wanna do the honors?"

Maxine grinned, her red hair swinging as she tucked the

letters around the tree. "It's crazy these are still so shiny after so long."

"Right?" Lexie laughed, joining me at the box and plucking an ornament the shape of a sparkly plane from inside. "Oh man, remember this? It was the year Chris got his pilot's license."

"Of course I do," I laughed. "I had to special order that thing online and the first one came broken a day before we were supposed to drive up. He was gutted. I must've gone to fifty stores to find a replacement before Quinn just glued it back together."

Something she acted like was a huge undertaking for her, but in reality I saw the easy smile that spread across her lips when we gave it back to him. It was always like that between her and him though.

Quinn, no matter what the situation, would do *anything* for him. I'd lost count of the times she'd driven Chris to and from the airport for his flights because the airport parking was criminally over priced. She would complain when she came back to our place, but would accept whatever imported sweets Chris got just for her as a thank you nonetheless.

Matt laughed, thumping Quinn on the shoulder. "Of course our resident artist saved the day. What did you bring this year Quinnie? A tattoo gun? A nipple piercing?"

Alex snorted a laugh, picking through the box and helping Lexie and I with decorating the tree. "Wait until you see mine. I think I really nailed the humble brag this year."

"Alright, alright. Hang on, I have to video chat Eric in— he'll be pissed if he misses the exchange. He even mailed me his so it'd get on the tree," Quinn muttered, pulling out her phone and starting a call.

I tried and failed not to feel bitter that she *did* actually know how to make a phone call while I pulled the little, red satin ribbon wrapped box out from where I'd hidden it near the fireplace.

The call connected and Quinn turned the phone around so that Eric could see everyone, a wide grin plastered over his face. "Merry Christmas ya filthy animals."

"Merry Christmas Eric, too cool to come hang with us this year?" Alex drawled, slinging an arm around Maxine's shoulders. It was almost so casual that any other onlooker wouldn't have batted an eyelash.

Lexie shot me a look that I returned meaningfully, using our best friend telepathy to say, 'Yeah, they wanna fuck each other.'

My best friend's eyes slipped towards Quinn and back and I shook my head.

Not doing that again.

"I want to go first!" called Max, pulling her ornament from her pocket—a snow globe shaped frame with a photo of Milo at its center, the words baby's first Christmas engraved into the silver metal. "To commemorate his first big holiday!" She shoved the ornament close to the camera before turning and proudly putting it on the tree.

Not that Milo cared, he was too busy snoring as he curled up to Quinn—despite the irritated looks that she was giving him.

"Me next!" chimed Matt, pulling out a glittery football from his suitcase stashed by the door. "First year that one of my client's won the Super Bowl!"

"Show-off," teased Alex, grabbing his own box from the sofa and opening it. Inside was a spaceship ornament, complete with little space man.

"Oh now who is bragging?" shouted Eric through the speaker.

"Hey, when you sell your proprietary micro-plastic eating bacteria to NASA then you can complain!"

Lexie snorted a laugh. "You guys, I swear to *God*. Here's mine." She slipped a little Eiffel Tower onto the tree. "First time one of my designs was printed in Vogue France."

"It's so much more prestigious than American Vogue!" we all shouted in unison, eye rolls aplenty. Lexie had talked about nothing else for the *entirety* of August.

Matt took the phone from Quinn and she gently dislodged Milo's from her lap.

"Me next!" Eric called and Quinn pulled a golden apple from the font of her bag. "Since I finally took the plunge and joined the rest of you losers in NYC this year."

"Yeah, with a six figure raise," snorted Lexie.

"What Lex, need a sugar daddy? All that Vogue France money dry up already?"

She stuck her tongue out at the phone in response but I didn't hear her reply. My ears were ringing the second I looked at the painted ornament Quinn pulled out next.

The familiar peaks of Mount Victoria and the icy, overly blue water of Lake Louise were hand painted on a circular piece of ceramic, a silhouette standing at its center. I could have sworn that—

Was that my picture?

Mount Victoria was not an unknown place per se ... but the silhouette in the middle was too unique to pass off as a mere coincidence.

A part of me wanted to brush off the suspicion that it was *my* picture that she had painted. After ignoring me for so long I wouldn't have expected her to keep up with what I posted on social media ... but the more I looked at it, the harder it was to ignore.

"This is gorgeous," complimented Alex. "Must've taken you forever."

"Nah," Quinn deflected, her eyes finding mine. She gave me sort of this wide eye'd stare. Like she'd been caught doing something wrong. "It was pretty last minute, actually."

She was lying. I could tell by the way she avoided my gaze.

I fiddled with the ribbon on the box in my hands, my cheeks heating. There was something uncomfortable settling in my chest, something that made me want to mention it. Maybe joke about it to ease the tension.

But then the moment passed, her ornament hung on the tree and Eric was back in her hands, everyone looking expectantly at me.

I opened the box taking out the first ornament inside, a key.

"Since I bought the townhouse," I said slowly, handing it to Lexie who put it on the tree as I pulled out the second occupant of the box with shaking fingers.

I held up a beautifully molded dove, its features painted with chromatic silver. On the side, it read; *For Chris, gone but not forgotten.*

Tears welled and I turned quickly, placing the ornament on the tree with my back to the now silent room. The whiplash of emotions was almost enough to cause my head to spin. On one hand, I couldn't even look Quinn in the eyes without feeling something I shouldn't, while the other was still the heavy weight of Chris's death.

What was wrong with me?

"That's really nice, Hazelnut," Max whispered.

I smiled weakly as I turned around, straightening my spine in an attempt not to look so pathetic.

"Group photo in front of the tree? Maybe I'll even let Robo Eric be in it."

Chapter 4

Quinn

She knew.

She *absolutely* fucking knew.

God this was so awkward. I knew I should've prepared better. Maybe thought through what to bring that wouldn't totally out my obsession to the entire group?

But even so, I couldn't get that damned picture of her out of my mind. It was stupid to paint a picture of *her* for the Christmas ornament, especially when we were here to reminisce about her dead fiancé.

Then when she looked at me ... there was a flash of recognition in her eyes and immediately, I knew she understood what the picture was.

And that's why, instead of going and mingling with everyone else in the kitchen, I went to bed. No one batted an eyelash when I excused myself to turn in early for the night, all of them too distracted by sharing the memories of this place *and* Chris.

I so badly wanted to sit there with them, remembering my friend. He had been such an important part of all of our lives—

of *my* life. And now every time I went about my day, I was hit with all the things we used to do together. Whether it be going to the same cafe that we used to visit after a night of heavy drinking because they had this *delicious* breakfast sandwich that seemed to chase away the hangover, or just driving around time and remembering all the times he occupied my passenger seat.

... But I just couldn't bring myself to sit there any longer.

I'm not sure if anyone felt my awkwardness whenever Chris and Hazel's relationship was brought up, but after the fifth time of someone mentioning how perfect they were together, I had to excuse myself.

Which meant when I woke up the next morning, it was well before everyone else. And since the hot water downstairs wasn't working, I was forced to use the bathroom in the hall upstairs.

A little time under the water would help me clear my head. Get me back on track.

I'd taken my time in the shower, trying to wash away my embarrassment from the gift that'd lingered even as the sun rose. But, the second I met my eyes in the fogged up mirror ... it came back full force.

Most of the steam had dissipated, leaving me with a perfect picture of my reddened face. Wet hair was stuck to my skin and droplets of water ran down my body towards the towel I'd hitched around my hips.

I was so fucking stupid.

"Get your shit together," I whispered to myself viciously.

I regretted coming here. It had only been a day for god's sake and I was already hiding out in the bathroom like a little girl.

You're here for Hazel. For Chris. You can set aside whatever it is that you still feel for her and just focus on what's good for her. You owe her that much.

Logically, I knew what I needed to do. I also knew that if I just stayed near Max and that smelly squishy dog, I wouldn't have time to even *think* about Hazel.

But the memories of our time together had started to play in the back of my mind, like the moment we came face to face the dam had broken, flooding my brain with nothing else.

The way her hands had felt as they gripped my face. Her soft lips and stroking tongue as it slid against mine. The desperate, needy little noises she made when she—

Stop being selfish.

With a sigh, I pulled the towel off and began to dry my hair. It muffled my hearing and caused the quiet, sleepy voices that'd started to float up from the kitchen to fade away, giving me time with my spiraling thoughts. But, it'd also muffled the sound of the door being pushed open.

I hadn't even realized that someone walked in on me until I felt the rush of cold wind slicing across my skin.

I pulled the towel off of my head and looked towards the door, thinking maybe it was someone walking by or that someone had turned the air on, but *no*—I was met with Hazel's green eyes, wide with surprise.

Her dark hair was pulled into the messy bun that she'd slept in, a few strands framing her face. Pretty pink lips popped open, a light blush dusting her cheeks. It was a delicious color that I couldn't help but want to see more of. Like summer-fresh strawberries.

I couldn't help but let my eyes wander to the pajamas she wore. I'd gotten a glimpse of them last night when she and the others were saying their goodnights—but now I had her all to myself and could greedily take in the sight before me.

She had on a cropped shirt that showed the majority of her

midriff, along with high waisted short-shorts trimmed with frills. The set was cute and showed a lot of skin. The black fabric topped with the pattern of strawberries, the very fruit called to mind only moments before.

They suited her perfectly.

It didn't help that she wasn't wearing a bra, her nipples peeking through the fabric tight with the cold; the sight of it brought me back to my own nudity.

My mind whirled as I thought of what to do.

We were friends, and more than that at times. She'd seen me naked over a dozen times. There was nothing to be shy about. If it was any other person I might have tried to nonchalantly hide myself or shot them a glare, but *Hazel?*

A part of me wanted her to see.

A part of me wanted to walk right up to her and just stand there, seeing if she would jump me like she had at the funeral.

A memory I'd tried all too hard to erase. But in that moment, with the two of us staring, all I could remember was the feeling of her lips against mine and her soft moans in my ear.

She slammed her mouth shut but didn't move from her spot. A flutter of excitement raced through me.

Slowly, I took a step towards her, throwing the towel over my shoulder.

"Did you need something?" I asked, leaning my arm on the wall beside her head.

She sucked in a sharp breath of air and took a startled half step back as I crowded her space, her eyes traveling all over.

"S-Sorry—I-I didn't mean to—I thought you were in your room and I-I—"

"If you wanted to join all you had to do was ask, *Haze*," I said, falling back into our old habits far too easy.

And it was *easy* between us back then, even when she was

with Chris. The banter—flirting, really—always came naturally to us and she would hit back even harder, sometimes making me flush. I missed it. I missed her. I'd give anything to get back there. To get rid of these violent feelings that were muddying the waters in our relationship.

But it was different this time. I should've known that, but for some reason between the time she opened the door and me leaning over her, I forgot why we were here.

That time had passed at all.

Or maybe, it was just that I *wanted* to forget about it. That I wanted to forget about everything outside of the bathroom, outside of this cabin. So maybe that's why I shook off all the voices in my head telling me to back off. Why I leaned in close enough I could practically taste her spearmint toothpaste.

I imagined her standing on tiptoes, getting as close as she could without our lips touching to deliver a snarky but flirty one liner that would make my head swoon and suck the air out of the room.

But she didn't.

Because that's not who she was anymore. Not since the funeral.

Her expression hardened and she cast me a look that caused a wave of guilt to hit me.

"Sorry, I..." But she didn't finish. Instead, she shut the door.

Like the day before, she left me staring after her.

Shit.

The guilt of it all hit me like a truck. Not just because of how Hazel had reacted, but knowing that I was doing this to Chris. His words from right before they got together ran rampant through my mind.

"You wouldn't mind, would you?" he asked. *"I know you two have history..."*

"*Not at all,*" I lied. "*I think you and Hazel would be good together. Perfect actually.*"

"*Good,*" he said with a light chuckle. "*Because she might be the girl I marry ...someday I mean.*"

And true to his words, he tried to. And almost made it. I'd stood by and watched as my two best friends fell in love and there was nothing I could do about it.

Because who was I to ruin their happiness?

He hasn't been dead for long and you're already making moves on his fiancee?

I leaned back against the counter with a loud sigh.

This trip is going to suck.

Hazel didn't look at me for hours after that—*moment*—between us.

Not when we were eating breakfast. Not when we were laughing and reminiscing about college. And certainly not when our friends announced that they would *all* be going out to get supplies.

It had been a unanimous decision that *all* of them would go and leave me and Hazel here. As if suddenly they all clocked into what was going on between us. Or more accurately, *me.* Apparently they'd decided it amongst themselves when Hazel and I had our moment in the bathroom, no doubt using that time to gossip about us.

I saw what they were doing.

Max and Matt may have been the most obvious. They were far too close, sending each other conspiratorial grins.

I almost wanted to spill it right there that she was vying to get under both Matt and Alex, just to watch as the drama unfolded.

But unlike them, I was good at keeping secrets.

For a lawyer, you would think he'd have a better poker face, but whatever he was thinking was written all over his expression. It was in the way his eyes lit up behind the thick lenses of his glasses and moved between the two of us, or how that beaming smile of his spread across his face.

"Go for it Quinnie, there's your shot. No need to thank me." I could hear that grating voice of his in my mind like he'd whispered directly in my ear; it only caused my irritation to skyrocket.

Max, on the other hand, was giving me the most obvious look. She was rooting for me, I knew she was. She was the only person who truly knew just how obsessed I'd been with Hazel.

At least they were taking the fucking dog with them.

I looked towards Alex in hope that he would be the one to show me some mercy only to be met with his stoic face giving me no indication that he was about to step in.

"Everyone?" Hazel's voice broke my staring contest with Alex. I turned to look at her as she leaned forward on the kitchen counter, placing her chin in her hand. She still hadn't changed out of those *fucking pajamas*, her bare legs like a siren call.

"Don't you worry Hazelnut," Matt said, his boisterous voice reverberating through the open concept room causing me to wince. "I promise to get you a chocolate bar while I'm there."

He topped it off with a wink.

Hazel scoffed.

I couldn't help but roll my eyes.

"Fine, *fine*," I said with a sigh, sensing the battle was already lost. "Just get more booze while you're at it. If I have to spend one more sleepless night with Alex's snoring I'm going to go insane."

Alex opened his mouth for a retort but Matt was already

there covering his mouth and dragging him towards the door, Lexie and Max close behind both with varying expressions of amusement.

"We'll be back soon kids!" Matt yelled as he pulled on his coat. "Don't do anything I wouldn't!"

I let out a sigh as soon as everyone filtered out of the house.

Somehow, I'd forgotten how exhausting they were all together. It was much better when there were only two or three of us at a time.

The shift of Hazel's slipper covered feet behind me reminded me that she was still here. I turned to look at her only to notice that she was staring at her phone. Ignoring me.

Great.

I thought of her reaction to me flirting with her earlier and immediately felt the need to apologize. I squashed the impulse as soon as it came up.

I did nothing wrong ... or at least that's what I tried to tell myself. It made the guilt easier to bear.

I wasted no time rummaging through the cabinets, trying to find anything to take the edge off. It was almost empty save for the few bags of powdered hot cocoa and some questionable canned goods. If someone told me they had been here since our last trip up, I'd believe them.

"Damn," I mumbled. "We really got nothing, huh?"

I turned to look at Hazel, expecting her to continue the conversation but she only shrugged; her eyes glued to the screen in her hand.

"Yep," she said, bringing us back to the one word territory.

Fucksakes.

I walked towards her, keeping the counter between us. It seemed like a good idea after earlier.

God I felt like a fucking teenager. One that couldn't control themselves around a pretty girl.

But this wasn't just any *pretty girl* it was *Hazel*.

She didn't try to hide her phone, giving me a front row seat to all of the pictures of her and Chris she had on her phone. She was swiping through a few, then pausing, before continuing onto the next ones.

At that point, I had to believe that she was doing this on purpose to get back at me for flirting earlier.

"Sucks that Eric couldn't come," I commented airily. "Has no respect for tradition."

If she thought I was going to apologize, she had another thing coming.

"It's probably busy this time of year for him," Hazel said, her eyes darting up to mine for just a moment before gluing them back to her phone. "Marketing and Christmas go hand in hand, after all. I worked sixteen hour days to pre schedule everything that needed to go live while I was here."

I made a noise of agreement and tried to look anywhere but at our dead friend—but I couldn't. I'd loved him once too, in my own way. Hearing about his diagnosis had gutted me in a way I never thought possible. We *all* lost him too soon, but having Hazel here, deteriorating in front of our eyes, it was like we were on the verge of losing her too.

"He would have been glad we got together," she murmured and went through three pictures at a time, ones that I was in with them as well.

"You think?" I asked, my mouth suddenly dry.

"Yeah, I'm glad that most people could show up."

Oh. Right. The cabin. Latin 101 Study Group. Not Hazel and I. Not us, us.

I nodded and swallowed thickly.

"It's the least we could do," I said, leaning on the countertop. Like she could sense our new closeness, she looked up at me. "For him and you. We ... worry about you, ya know?"

A smile spread across her face. To anyone else, it would look like the picture perfect smile, but I could see the pain behind it.

"No one has to worry about me," she said and locked her phone. "I've been fine. Moving on, just like everyone else."

I chewed on my bottom lip, unsure what to say. Because it wasn't just like *everyone else*... Everyone else had time to prepare for his death, to really get to say goodbye, but Hazel...

"It's okay ... to not move on as well," I said finally, the words coming out clumsy and awkward.

I wanted her to know that we understood that she was still suffering because of his death and none of us blamed her for it.

"I did," she said, her voice raising an octave. "I *am*. I'm good, Quinn. You don't need to worry."

I nodded and turned to look back into the kitchen. I couldn't stand the way her eyes looked as she tried to fool me with that smile.

Was she lying to me or to herself?

It made my chest clench and my throat swell.

"Hot cocoa?" I asked, mostly to put some space between us.

"Please," she said with a relieved sigh, probably happy to have the conversation behind us.

At least we could agree on one thing.

Chapter 5

Hazel

I settled onto the sofa with the hot chocolate Quinn made, putting on one of those frivolous feeling Hallmark holiday movies as background noise while I edited some pictures from the night before on my phone.

Anything to keep my hands busy, really. Because if I was left idle for half a second I was liable to:

1. Jump Quinn after that little peep show.
2. Keep making a total idiot of myself by trying and failing to talk about Chris in a way that didn't make me seem like I was still totally obsessed with him.

I ran a hand over the messy knot I'd pulled my hair into, sighing.

Did she have to be so ... Quinn all the time? It was impossible to understand what the fuck she was thinking. Seriously, you ignore me for a whole damn year and then—*What*? I accidentally walk in on you—you absolutely flirt with me—and then you want to act like nothing happened?

I took a sip of my hot chocolate, balancing my phone on my knees as I held the mug with both hands.

Stupid. Sexy. *Perfect* Quinn.

She'd even put cinnamon in my cup—even though I knew she thought it was gross.

How could someone know every intimate detail about you and yet be a stranger at the same time?

I looked over to the L of the couch where she was huddled, dressed now in an oversized t-shirt and pants that swallowed up the soft curves but left her muscular biceps out for the entire world to bask in. They practically had me drooling on the tile a few hours before when I first caught sight of them.

She had clearly been taking care of herself far better than I had in the past few months.

A thought that caused the slightest bit of bitterness to rise up in me.

Snow had started falling before everyone left, Lexie cheekily taking the time to text me that now would be a great time to talk to Quinn the second we were left alone.

But I could barely look at her, much less talk to her. Not without picturing the way she gasped when my tongue—

"It's really starting to come down," Quinn said in a bored tone, looking out the window. "You think they'll be back soon?"

"Hopefully," I replied, shaking the memory from my mind. "I forgot to grab the snacks out of Lexie's car last night so we are kinda stuck with whatever is left from breakfast until they get back. Well, except those." I pointed to the tin of cookies I brought, now sitting on the low coffee table.

"I think Matt and Alex put some stuff in the fridge too. Want me to see if I can make us some lunch?"

"Nah, it's fine." I set my cocoa down and pulled the fluffy throw from the back of the couch, spreading it over my lap. I scrolled my phone for a bit as we sat in tense silence. Though I had a feeling Quinn was pretending to ignore me as much as I was pretending to ignore her.

Hyper aware of every one of her tiny movements on the other end of the couch.

Don't be fucking weird. Just ... say something. Anything.

"I really liked your ornament," I blurted.

The tips of Quinn's ears flushed pink. "It was last minute, I wasn't sure if—"

"If you were going to come?" I interrupted, clicking my phone screen off and tossing it onto the table.

"Yeah," she said, like that ended the conversation.

But it *didn't* end the conversation, not until she told me why she'd iced me out the last year. So what, we got a little drunk at the funeral and hooked up—Chris would've thought it was funny. *Ironic* even. Probably would have made a joke about how it was only a matter of time. It's not like we were subtle about hooking up before I got with him.

It wasn't me who didn't want to commit—I wasn't the reason we broke it off.

But just like in college, it was me who was left with a broken heart because of it.

Hurricane Quinn never failed to leave a wave of destruction in her path.

At least she was consistent.

The fire crackled in the grate as the lovers decorated a Christmas tree on the screen. The silence between us mounted the longer that Quinn sketched and I pretended like I still cared about the movie at all. But no matter how much I tried to focus, her presence never lessened and my thoughts just got louder and louder.

Maybe *I* was an asshole. How many girls screwed their

dead fiancé's best friend when they weren't even in the ground yet?

I loved Chris. I did. But a part of me always loved Quinn too. And that one had been around much longer than Chris. Loving her had become like a habit. It was familiar to me and easy to fall back into when it was just us shielded by the walls of the cabin.

If this was one of those books that Max was obsessed with I would've gotten to have them both, but real life didn't work like that. Fate and fucking colon cancer made that decision for me in the end. And instead of having one, the other, or both, I was left with *no one.*

I stood from the couch, unable to sit and pretend like I wasn't dying to look at her anymore.

"I'm going for a nap. Wake me up when everyone is back."

"Yeah," Quinn grunted, not bothering to look up.

It was just as well, I felt like she was looking through me half the time anyway. Even when she was flirting, it was like there was a chasm between us that I couldn't cross.

Quinn and I. Not us.

I grabbed my phone and abandoned my half full hot chocolate to head up the stairs to the master bedroom I'd claimed as my own. The sheets were cold when I slid between them and I shivered, curling up under the duvet and shutting my eyes tight.

When I woke up, everyone would be back and we could go back to being strangers.

It's what Quinn wanted anyway.

A constant, irritating buzzing pulled me out of my dreams, sweet with gingerbread cookies and heady, soft kisses from

Quinn. I rolled onto my back, grabbing my phone from under my pillow and bringing it to my ear.

"'Lo?" I mumbled, still half asleep.

"How are things going with Quinn?" Lexie asked by way of greeting.

I groaned and I could practically hear Lexie wince.

"That good huh?"

"Yeah, are you guys almost back? I could use a buffer."

"Well ... about that." Lexie's voice was nervous as it came through the speaker, dousing my sleepy, post nap state in icy water.

"What?"

"It's a white out, the roads aren't safe. We're going to have to get a hotel in town for the night."

My heart dropped to my stomach and an ice cold panic filled my veins.

"Say sike right now Lex."

"Girl, I wish I c–"

"Hazzzzeeeeeeeelll!" Matt sang through the phone. "You lovebirds make up yet?"

"Put her on speaker!" Max whined in the background.

My lips popped open in surprise. "Matt, I'm going to kill you."

"You'll have to get in line." Alex laughed. "Quinn was giving those murdery stare vibes when we left too."

"You guys are all safe?" I asked, staring up at the wooden ceiling and wishing it would cave in so that I wouldn't have to deal with a whole night alone together.

For all their excitement, I wouldn't have put it past them to have found some sort of way to bring on this hellish snow storm just so that we would be forced to talk.

"Absolutely," Lexie promised.

"Okay, I'll see you all tomorrow then?"

"Yep, try not to kill each other before then," Alex called.

"Or if you do the murdering, I can refer you to a good criminal lawyer. It would be out of my field," Matt joked.

I sighed and disconnected the call, pulling the pillow over my face to scream until all the air was out of my lungs.

Just my fucking luck. What was already going to be a tense, if not downright uncomfortable week with Quinn was now a solo trip with my ex-best friend who'd spent the last year dodging my calls.

I slipped from bed, tossing the pillow onto the mattress before rooting through my bag for an oversized cable-knit sweater. I pulled it on, the warm cream colored wool hitting me at mid thigh and slipping a little over my shoulder as I padded out of the room in my slippers.

"Quinn?" I called as I took the stairs on stiff legs.

The woman in question was lounging on the sofa where I'd left her, my unfinished cup on her side of the table and thoroughly drank.

Didn't like cinnamon my butt.

She was snoring softly, lifts parted and her sketchbook sitting open beside her. I tried and failed not to snoop, picking the book up and turning it over to look at what she'd been working on.

Flowers spilled over the page like a waterfall, their petals soft and buoyant even in the preliminary stages of her line work.

I closed the sketchbook and carefully sat it on the table when movement caught my eye.

Quinn had adjusted in her sleep, the blanket I'd been curled in before pulled up under her chin.

Subconsciously my hand found my heart, rubbing over the spot that'd started to ache the second I'd seen her again.

After a year of dreaming about her full lips, the way they

turned down just slightly into a sort of permanent frown that is only more devastating when she smiled. Her dark eyebrows, contrasting with her fair peachy skin and blonde curls that I wanted to—

I gave into the impulse, carding my fingers through her hair with a feather light touch.

Fuck, no. There it was. The desperate longing I'd been trying to stamp out since she hadn't even bothered to text me on my birthday. I knew how stupid it was. She'd made herself perfectly clear. She didn't want me.

But it never made me stop needing her.

Before I could get too lost in my own pathetic fantasy I stepped back, quickly checking my face for tears before nudging her shoulder. "Quinn, b—" I cut myself off before the rest of the word *babe* could pass my lips. A year ago, even two, it would have been natural. But now? Not a chance.

It was dangerous to feed into the fantasy that it could be again. Even if it seemed like the cabin filtered out the real world ... it wouldn't for long. I had to remember that outside of here, she would never have reached out. She would have never taken the initiative to rekindle the relationship my heart so desperately seemed to crave.

Quinn mumbled unintelligibly in her sleep, her straight, slightly upturned nose scrunching adorably as she woke. Her blue eyes, so like the color of Lake Louise—the place she'd painted on that fucking ornament—opened blearily to meet mine.

"S'ok?" She slurred and I grinned despite my tortured inner monologue.

Sleepy Quinn, even when I was hurt and pissed and whatever else, was still the best Quinn.

"A blizzard rolled in. They can't drive back to us until tomorrow."

Quinn blinked, sitting up straighter. "What? It was barely snowing when you went upstairs!" She turned, looking out the window where the snow was coming down so hard it was practically horizontal in the wind. "Fuck."

"Yup," I said, flopping down on the sofa beside her, careful not to touch. "Looks like it's just us for tonight."

Chapter 6

Quinn

Stay calm. *Stay fucking calm, Quinn.*

They'll be back tomorrow. It's okay. We'll survive. Hazel and I. *Alone.* In the cabin.

It should be just fine.

If I could forget how much I wanted her back in the bathroom. It had been years since we were intimate on a regular basis, the time at the funeral had been a one off ... but that didn't stop all the images of us fucking each other's brains out every chance we got back in college running through my mind.

Fuck, I'd even dreamed about it.

One minute I'd been watching as Hazel stood in front of me, taking off one of those skimpy two piece matching sets she fucking *loves*—leaving the so called clothes on the floor—before straddling my lap and pulling my mouth to hers, and the next I'd woken up to those same green eyes.

It took me a moment to realize that the Hazel in front of me *was not* the one from my dream and that I probably shouldn't grab hold of her to continue where we'd left off.

It'd been another hour since we'd heard the news and it was

quickly becoming awkward again. Or maybe it was just me. Hazel had plopped down on the couch next to me, scrolling aimlessly through social media while I attempted to focus on client work.

The thigh piece wasn't due for another few weeks, but I had nothing else to keep my mind busy. And I sure as hell wasn't opening any of my social media right next to her on the off chance that she saw how much I'd been stalking her.

Just as the thought went through my head my phone buzzed in my pocket. I pulled it out, catching a notification that caused my heart to slam against my ribcage.

TrippinWithHaze tagged you in a photo!

I turned to Hazel slowly, finding her eyes already trained in my direction with a smirk curving her lips that made my insides heat.

"You didn't," I glowered.

"I so *did*," she said with a soft giggle that caused my chest to ache and my breathing to stop entirely.

It was so ... familiar. I'd heard the noise a thousand times over the years but still, even after so long, it felt just the same. Like my favorite song and a sip of high quality gin rolled into one.

With a shaky hand I opened Instagram to Hazel's most recent update, she'd labeled it as a '*photo dump*' and posted a bunch of pictures I hadn't even seen her take.

The first one was of her, probably right before Max and I arrived. There was snow in her hair and she was holding a mug of hot cocoa with a blanket on her shoulders. Her cheeks and nose perfectly reddened as she laughed.

The following photos were of the lake's beautiful scenery, a blurry mirror photo of her holding up a peace sign, the fireplace, a close up of mine and Matt's ornaments on the tree, and last but not least—me.

Well, of my arm and drawing at least. A perfectly framed shot of my forearm and sketchbook, cut off where the sleeve of my crewneck was pushed to my elbow.

I'd been so focused on trying *not* to notice her the last hour that I had totally missed when she took it. I couldn't be mad at it. It was a good photo that showed off my tattoos and artwork. One that I might even take for myself.

The issue was the followers I had gotten because of it. An almost constantly changing number in the upper right hand corner of my screen. There were so many notifications that when I tried to open the tab my entire phone froze and was stuck on the photo.

I closed my eyes and let out a heavy, frustrated sigh.

"My followers are curated for people who want to book me, Haze," I mumbled.

I wasn't the best at social media—it had taken me *forever* to get the half decent following I had—and there was Hazel, snapping her fingers and getting me thousands of followers in seconds. It was almost ... demeaning.

Not to mention that I *had* tried to curate my followers in a way where I knew they were interested in *me*. Not because of some endorsement from an influencer. Or because of whatever the gossips thought was going on between us.

"Are you seriously complaining that I *gave* you *free advertisement?*" she asked, scowling.

"I can't even get out of the app!" I snapped, showing her the frozen screen.

She rolled her eyes. "That's why you turn off notifications."

Finally, the app closed by itself. My phone was still vibrating like crazy, a never ending ping from constant notifications. When I opened Instagram again I saw that not only were people following me in droves, but they'd also started to comment on my photos.

Especially the rare ones that had my face in them.

> DANIIORTEGA: OMG, YOU THINK THEY'RE
> FUCKING?
>
> ELLEMAE: IT'S A SOFT LAUNCH! WATCH IN HER
> NEXT POST THEY WILL MAKE IT OFFICIAL!
>
> BABYD0LL4369: IS ANYONE ELSE CONFUSED AT
> WHO TF THIS PERSON IS?
>
> SUNNS4LTXX: WAIT, SINCE WHEN IS SHE GAY?
>
> AUTHORBEXDEVEAU: OH, SO SHE IS GAY GAY.

"Come on Quinn, it's not *that* bad," Hazel said as she crawled over to me, her cable-knit sweat slipping off her shoulder and giving me the urge to *bite*. She peered over my shoulder as I scrolled through the notifications.

"This will look bad for both of us, Haze," I growled and looked towards her. I hadn't realized how close her face was until I turned.

I just needed to lean forward a couple inches and—

Her eyes widened when our gazes met. "How so?"

I could *taste* the hot cocoa on her breath ... or maybe it was the lingering taste of her from the dream. Either way, I was already lost in her.

I saw everything.

The way her eyes fell to my lips. The way her breath hitched. The way her tongue licked her glossed lips.

Don't make this worse for yourself Quinn. She's grieving.

My mind was always the logical one. It was too bad it was my body that was reacting. We were alone, for the first time since the funeral. The feeling of her skin on mine and the taste of her seared into my memory—every fiber of my being pushing me closer to her.

To the girl that made my world stop.

The hand that held my phone dropped it and slowly trailed along the leather of the couch cushion, until my arm rested on the back of the couch. I was careful not to touch her, but the move made it so I was almost holding her. If she so much as breathed in too deeply we'd be touching.

"Quinn," she whispered, her hand finding my knee.

I couldn't help myself. I leaned closer, my eyes falling to her lips.

"Don't move," I commanded softly.

So close. We were so, *so* close.

My other hand circled her wrist, slowly started the path up her arm. I was sure, based on the way she shivered that under the wool, goosebumps had erupted along her skin.

"Plea—" Hazel started as darkness fell over us, the subtle hum of the electronics throughout the cabin grinding to a sudden, deafening silence.

The fucking power had gone out.

"Are you fucking *kidding me?*"

I let out a small sigh of relief as the pan of soup simmered.

Luckily, the cabin was outfitted with a gas stove so—with the help of Alex's lighter, Hazel had found with the packet of cigarettes he *definitely* didn't smoke anymore—I was able to start one of the burners.

The entire house's power had gone out and it was completely dark now. Almost instantly the cold started to seep in and whatever was happening between Hazel and I had been completely stomped out.

Maybe it was for the best.

But even so, it didn't stop me from dreading this whole thing. If anything, it was worse because now Hazel and I were even more uncomfortable with each other than before.

And it was all my fault.

She was in the living room, trying to start a fire while I scrounged around for something to turn into a half decent meal. There was no way we'd both make it out of here alive while we were ... whatever we were *and* hungry.

The others weren't kidding when they said we needed supplies, but no one thought to bring anything other than canned soup and tuna? Out of the six grown ass adults that came?

If I was being honest, my anger came from the fact that Hazel and I were interrupted. It seemed like nature was against us here. Maybe it was a sign that I should get my head in the game and stop daydreaming about someone who was still so obviously hung up on her ex.

Not her ex, I reminded myself. *They didn't break up. He fucking died.*

"Is it ready?" Hazel called from the other room.

I bit my tongue to stop the snappy remark I wanted to deliver her.

"Not yet," I called back.

"I can't get the fire to start," she said from the other room, her voice tight with frustration. "Can we switch?"

I had to close my eyes to stop myself from exploding.

Deep breaths Quinn.

In ... then out...

The shuffle of her slipper-clad feet against the kitchen's tile had my head snapping towards her, Hazel had her arms crossed over her chest and she was shivering.

When her eyes met mine I froze. We were so close to kissing in the other room. I'd wanted it more than anything in that moment. I didn't care about the social media post. I didn't care that the power was out.

All I wanted was to pick up where we left off. I couldn't

help but wonder what she had thought about when I leaned in close.

Did she want it too? Did she remember how easy it used to be between us? Did she think of me as much as I thought about her?

Or... or did she think of Chris?

I couldn't hold her gaze.

Of course she thought of Chris.

Just like in the bathroom, I hadn't been thinking of Hazel, only my own selfish *wants*.

Guilt racked my body and suddenly, no matter how much I had wanted to be with Hazel, I had the strongest desire to just throw myself out with the snow. That was when the anger seeped in.

But it wasn't anger with Hazel. It was all on me.

It was because *I* couldn't move on when literally everyone else had. I'd become way too selfish when I should have been thinking of Hazel's feelings.

"Go change your clothes," I said, noticing she was still wearing practically nothing while I'd doubled up sweaters and put on a heavier pair of sweatpants as soon as the power shut off.

There were small candles in the emergency kit we found, and though they offered a little light, it still left a majority of the room in darkness.

She crossed the kitchen and nudged me out of the way to take over the soup.

"Please," she said. "Just do it. Once the fire is going I'll be fine."

I was frozen to my spot. I knew I should go into the living room and do as she asked, but my worry for her overshadowed reason.

That worry quickly turned into anger.

"*Hazel*," I said harshly. "Go change. It's *freezing* and we don't know how long the power will be out so I need you to get your cute ass upstairs before it freezes off."

"You think I'm cute?" There was a slight teasing to her tone, one that was threatening to send me over the edge.

Cheeky brat.

"Go, *now*."

Her head whipped around and I was met with a glare.

"Don't order me around, *Quinn*."

"I wouldn't have to if you would've just been smart about this in the first place," I said, maneuvering her away from the stove. "Go. *Now*."

Her forest green eyes widened in shock as if she couldn't believe that I was asking her to take care of herself.

"It'll take you literally two minutes to—"

"Can you just take care of yourself for five seconds, Hazel?" I asked, exasperated.

Images of the dark circles I'd caught under her makeup and far to skinny body flashed through my mind. I was angry, *hurt*, that she'd been wasting away. That the girl that I lo—*cared for*—had stopped caring about herself while all I could do was worry about her from the sidelines.

"You don't sleep. You probably don't eat. How long has it been since you did something for yourself that wasn't in the name of social media?" I let out a scoff. "Sorry, '*work*'. You can't even put extra clothes on when you're about to freeze to death. In case you've forgotten, we are in a blizzard in the middle of fucking *nowhere* with *no one* in the near vicinity that can help us. Just do what you're fucking told!"

I hadn't realized I was shouting until it was far too late, I slammed my mouth shut as soon as the words were out, wishing I could take them back.

Fuck. Way to fucking go Quinn.

I knew I should have just walked away. It was just a goddamn fire. She would have changed in a few minutes anyway.

"Oh so *now* you care?" Hazel exploded, letting out a bitter laugh. "You haven't seen me for *eleven* months. You *completely* ghosted me after the funeral and now *all of the sudden* you *care* about how *I'm* doing Quinn?"

I swallowed thickly and took a step back. Guilt rushed through me so viciously it caused my head to spin.

"I'm sorry," I whispered. "I shouldn't have said that. Let me just go—"

"Go what?" she shouted. "Run away? That's a staple for you isn't it? Just fucking off when things get tough? Or maybe you rubbed the two brain cells in that pumpkin head of yours together and realized that your actions fucked me up as much as—as—" She swallowed hard, tears brimming in her eyes. "Is it too much for you, huh? To have to face the consequences of your own actions?" She took a step closer to me, invading my space. I couldn't hold her angry gaze as those vibrant green eyes tore into me, peeling the skin clear off my bones and scooping my heart out into her tiny, shaking hands.

"Haze, let's not—"

"I lost my *fiancé*, Quinn," she spat. "I lost *everything* and you couldn't even pick up the damn phone because you're too much of a fucking coward. It's always been this way. Every time even an ounce of feelings were involved you run away. Aren't you tired of it? Aren't you ashamed? Doesn't it get lonely, not being able to find someone who can put up with it five years after we broke up?" She laughed, a high, semi-hysterical noise that threatened danger. "Oh right we didn't *break up* because according to you we were *never together in the first place!*"

The only sound was Hazel's hard breathing and the wind

howling outside. The silence between us stretching and twisting until it was unbearable, cutting through me like her words and leaving invisible wounds that bled onto the hardwood.

The worst part was that she wasn't *wrong*. I did run when things got serious. It was *me* who couldn't commit to anyone ... to *her*. Who was I to judge how she grieved someone who was able to give her what she needed? Especially if I wasn't there to help her.

Without another word I turned on my heel and stalked into the living room, my ears ringing.

"Just like I fucking thought," Hazel sniffed.

I wished I could prove her wrong, but I wasn't that person.

Fuck, I missed Chris. He would know exactly what to say right now.

I rubbed my wet eyes on my sleeve, frustration and shame swirling in my stomach.

Step one, get this fire lit. Step two, figure out how to fix things with Hazel. I'd clearly fucked up.

Chapter 7

Hazel

I'd sloshed half the soup onto the floor in one of my more childish moments. I was so frustrated that when I threw the wooden spoon back into the pot I knocked it off balance, meaning that a good third of the pot was spreading over the tiles.

Smooth move Haze, you fucking asshole.

I dragged my hands down my face, blowing out a frustrated breath. My throat was tight with unshed tears, but I'd told myself I wasn't going to cry on this trip and goddamn it, I wasn't going to do it.

It wasn't that I regretted saying that stuff to her, she had no right to tell me what to do after spending the last year acting like I didn't fucking exist. But maybe my delivery could have used some work.

I stooped down, cleaning up the spilled soup with a dishrag and putting what I could salvage back on the burner. It was gross and Quinn would have a fit if she found out, but there was no choice.

Not my finest moment. Especially since we had extremely limited resources until our friends got back to us tomorrow. With that in mind, I combed through the cabinets, finding a significant amount of dust, tacky holiday mugs, and a few more canned items that likely expired in 2017.

Deciding to save my pride, I headed up to my borrowed bedroom to find some sweat pants and lick my wounds in private. I dressed quickly, trading out my shorts for a loose pair of joggers and some thick socks.

See Quinn? I can take care of myself!

I shoved my shorts back into my luggage, a curious dull thud sounding as the weight of my bag shifted. I pulled the suitcase to the side curiously, my hands traveling over the floorboards until I found the loose one, pulling it up to reveal a hidden alcove in the floor.

I reached my hand in, coming into contact with fabric, invisible in the darkness of the hole. Grabbing hold tightly, I yanked a duffle bag through the missing plank with a little wiggling. It was heavy and a little dusty, but had an air of mystery that I simply couldn't deny.

The call of adventure was too much for me to turn down. Besides, we were in serious need of some Christmas magic. I was using my phone as a damn flashlight in what should be considered an incredibly comedic situation if Quinn and I could just manage to set aside our differences for a few hours.

I unzipped the bag, rummaging through its contents with the help of the light from my phone screen. Inside was a bottle of fancy aged whiskey, snacks, playing cards, and—most shocking of all—a pack of cigarettes. I laughed, dropping to my butt on the rapidly cooling wood.

"Fucking *Chris* and his goddamn hidey holes."

Of course he'd left some surprises around the cabin for us

to find, as if the ones that littered our loft in Manhattan hadn't been filled to the brim with little notes and treats that I'd found for months after he was gone.

Shaking my head, I shoved everything back into the bag, slinging it over my shoulder and heading downstairs to try and turn what was left of our meal into something edible.

By the time I was done, Quinn had settled back on the couch with her drawing. Her hoodie was off now, leaving her in a shirt that showed off her tattoos. And her ample biceps.

Feeling a little bad about drooling over her while we were still fighting, I headed into the kitchen. I made quick work of fixing her a bowl of soup and a fairly bland tuna sandwich. I even took the time to fix her another cup of hot cocoa—cinnamon free.

I cleared my throat a little awkwardly, setting the bowl of soup, sandwich, and hot chocolate onto the coffee table in front of her. She looked up at me, her gaze guarded.

It took me a moment to bring my own, less full bowl over—which I ignored in favor of my spiked hot chocolate. I needed just a touch of liquid courage if I was going to get what I needed to say out.

Quinn leaned forward, taking up the mug in her hands and bringing it to her lips. Recognition flared in her crystalline eyes and she smiled, almost like she couldn't help it. "What's this?"

"I found us a little treat upstairs, there are some snacks too —but I figured you'd want those later."

She snorted. "Fucking Chris."

"Yup," I sighed, leaning back against the squashy sofa cushions.

Now that the fire had been lit it was damn cozy, though we'd need to sleep in the living room tonight. There wasn't nearly enough heat to travel all the way to our rooms upstairs.

"Haze, listen—"

"Can we just ... not? I'm tired of not talking about it as much as I'm tired of talking about it. I'm sure you had your reasons to keep away. I know you loved him too." I bit my lip, looking at the steaming cup in my hands. "Just be here now, okay? I—" I swallowed hard, forcing the next words out despite the way my mouth fought not too. "I missed you."

"I missed you too," Quinn muttered, taking a long drink from her mug. "I'm sorry for yelling."

"You're bossy as ever," I teased.

"And you're just as damn stubborn."

"Guilty." I grinned, trading my cup for the bowl of soup. It was warm and tasted adjacently like chicken, which was about as many nice things as I'd found to say about it when Quinn scooched across the cushions towards me. Close enough I could feel her body heat.

"Are you warm enough?"

"Yeah, I'm good. Eat or you'll be hangry and we're just going to argue again."

"I do not get *hangry*," she snapped and I raised an eyebrow in response. "Oh shut up, Haze." She took up her soup, shoveling spoonfuls into her mouth like it'd insulted her mother.

We ate in companionable and slightly less awkward silence. There was still a lot unsaid between us—like 'hey Quinn, I haven't stopped thinking about you for months and even though I think I'm ready to start dating now I've turned down every invite for ages because it feels like something is unfinished between us'—but right now didn't seem like the time to address it.

Or the naked bathroom moment.

Or the almost kiss.

It was almost a kiss, right?

When the soup and sandwiches were gone we moved our dishes to the sink, using snow from the bank outside to chill our whiskey as we played cards to pass the time.

"Want to up the ante a bit?" I asked, sliding my cards over the table top with two fingers.

"What do you mean?"

"Remember the Delta Phi spring mixer sophomore year?"

"Strip poker?" Quinn choked around a sip of her drink. "Are you crazy? It'll be col—"

"The fire's on, it's warm, and if you're so worried about getting cold you better win."

She rolled her eyes. "Fine, but if you get hypothermia it's your own fault."

"As if," I sneered, the alcohol we'd drank warming my insides and dulling my anxiety enough that I didn't blush as I met Quinn's hungry eyes. "I hope you're ready to lose your shirt."

I wasn't half bad at cards. But if my barely concocted and whiskey addled plan was to come together I needed to lose a few hands. Which also meant dealing with Quinn's insufferable poor-winning.

Twenty minutes later, I was suffering through *exactly* that.

"What was that about losing my shirt?" Quinn asked, running a hand through her dirty blonde curls.

I bit my lip, fluttering my eyelashes at her. "All in due time."

Never mind the fact that I'd had three of a kind and threw them away that hand. I didn't have the balls to flat out tell Quinn anything, especially not while she was still acting like *that*. But she was always weak when it came to bare midriff and a bit of cleavage.

"Oh yeah?" she challenged back as I stood, making a show

out of slipping out of my sweater. Underneath I still had on the little strawberry printed pajama top from before, sans bra. Despite my assurances that with the fire we'd be warm and the whiskey in my veins my nipples were hard against the fabric.

I dropped the sweater to the floor with a soft thud of fabric meeting wood, flourishing my hand. "Your move, babe."

Chapter 8

Quinn

Babe.

The word circled through my head and caused a light feeling to bubble up inside my chest. I wanted to hear it again. How long had it been since we'd been close enough for pet names?

Had she realized what she just called me?

Her expression gave no indication that she did. Or at least that it wasn't a surprise that she'd said it. It made me question everything I'd thought back in the kitchen. It made me want to do selfish things again.

Like flirting back or even leaning over this counter and kissing her until she begged me to come up for air.

Shit.

I couldn't tear my eyes from her. Not only did the pet name do things to me, but she was wearing that top again. The one with the cute little strawberries that showed her midriff.

God, I loved that set. I couldn't even be mad that she was still wearing those clothes under and so *obviously* cheating.

I didn't care about any of it. The guilt and hate seemed to

melt away leaving us in our own little bubble. It excited me, probably more than it should have.

Maybe ... it would be okay to be selfish just this once, while no one was around.

She raised her brow at me when I'd stared just a bit too long.

"Cat got your tongue?" she asked in that flirty tone of hers that did things to my heart and stomach and everywhere else.

She was doing this on purpose. She *had* to be.

But it was okay because no matter how hard my heart was pounding in my chest or how sweaty my palms got, *this* Hazel I understood well.

With a brush of confidence I reached forward and grabbed the edge of her barstool, pulling her toward me with a jerk. She let out a gasp as she tried to steady herself on the edge of the counter, fingers curling around the butcher block.

I pulled her legs between mine and closed mine around hers, effectively trapping her. Just touching Hazel shouldn't have sent such a thrill through me, but I couldn't suppress the shiver after seeing how her eyes widened and how those pink, impossibly kissable lips popped open in surprise.

"Don't want you to get cold, Haze," I purred in a low voice, sitting up straight.

She recovered quickly, a dangerous smirk pulling at her lips.

"Don't get too cocky just yet," she teased. "If I didn't know any better I would think that you're just delaying the inevitable. Trying to *distract* me."

I couldn't stop the smile that spread across my face. I leaned closer to her, enjoying the warmth radiating off her skin. We were far enough from the fireplace that the cold should have been bothering us by now, but the heat stirring between us was enough to keep my body comfortably warm.

"Is it working?" I asked.

Her eyes widened for a moment before she let out a laugh, but it was slightly forced and with the way her eyes lingered on me, I *knew* it was.

It's okay to be selfish, just this once. To think that maybe there was a part of her, underneath the mask she gave everyone, that wanted me as much as I wanted her.

"Nope," she said hastily. "Your turn still."

I made a show of rolling my eyes and went, laying the pair of jacks onto the countertop.

"Two of a kind."

Hazel smirked, slapping down three sevens.

"Fuck."

"That's right! Shirt off," Hazel said, a triumphant gleam in her emerald eyes.

With a sigh, I placed my cards on the table and shrugged out of my t-shirt. The cold air hit me with a vengeance, but the look on Hazel's face when she realized that I wasn't wearing a bra was enough to make it more than worth it.

I picked my cards back up and leaned back in my chair, giving her a prime view of my erect nipples. I spread my legs enough to give her some space but she kept hers pushed together, her eyes fixed to my chest.

"Don't act like you haven't seen it before," I said and took my time to let my own gaze roam her bare skin while she was otherwise distracted by my tits.

When her eyes finally met mine I had to hold in my breath. The tension between us skyrocketed and made it hard to breathe. Like a rubber band fit to snap.

Slowly, Hazel put down two of her cards. A pair of threes.

I couldn't help but smile, matching her speed I threw down my pair of tens.

"Why don't you make it even?" I asked, dropping my voice.

I reached forward and pulled at the small top. It was elastic and stretched too easily, giving me a glorious view down the front. It felt like I was crossing a line, but she didn't slap my hand away. I licked my lips as her erect nipples came into sight. It was only for a second, but it made my throat close and heat to rise in my belly.

I let the material fall back against her as she shimmied out of her joggers. She hadn't kept the shorts.

Then, in a moment, she was down to her socks, barely-there top, and see-through white panties. I could have sworn that they had cherries on them, but maybe it was the dark just playing tricks on my eyes.

Either way, all thoughts of poker were long gone from my mind.

"You could've taken your socks off," I murmured, letting my hand wander across her bare skin. She shivered at the contact and opened her legs just enough so my thumb could brush across her inner thigh.

I was one hundred percent taking it too far now.

My brain screamed at me to pull back, told me to end the game right this instant ... but I couldn't. And frankly, I didn't want to.

"I could have," she admitted, her voice hardly a whisper.

It sent a shiver down my spine.

Her skin was raised with goosebumps. I used both hands to run them up her thighs, taking advantage of being able to touch her again.

"You're cold," I murmured, my eyes locked on hers. "Should we stop?"

I didn't realize I was leaning forward until I was close enough to feel her breath skate across my cheek.

My hands followed her body, trailing up her thighs to circle her hips. I flexed my fingers, nearly moaning when her hands rested chastely on my chest.

"There's nothing else to do," she reasoned. "I'm enjoying myself just fine. I don't want to stop the game."

"And if I do?" I asked, letting my fingers tease at the lace band on the top of her panties before finding her waist. Her sharp intake of breath caused my mind to go blank save for the need to lean forward to kiss her.

It was insane. The hold she had on me. It didn't matter if it was during finals week in college, her fiancé's funeral, or even in the middle of a fucking snow storm. I would drop everything to feel her skin against mine again.

"Then you'll lose," she promised, tilting her head to the side to look at me through her lashes. "And never get to see what's underneath."

I couldn't look at her as I brushed my thumb across her nipple, the thin fabric did nothing to hide the peaked bud. Hazel shifted in her seat, her lower lip snagging between her teeth.

"Then we'll just have to work around it," I purred.

Her hands flying into my hair was the thing that finally snapped the thread holding me back.

I leaned into her, letting my lips trail her neck.

Fuck, her skin was so *soft*.

"If you want me to stop you should say something," I said, using my free hand to hike her leg around my hips. It was an awkward angle because of how we were sitting, forcing her to bend her knee, but it gave me perfect access to the cute little scrap of white fabric screaming my name.

She let out a light whimper as I ran my tongue down the expanse of her throat.

When I leaned back to look at her, her face was flushed,

mouth slightly open for her panting breaths. The hunger in her eyes was exhilarating.

There was no going back now.

"What are we doing?" she asked.

I pinched her nipple lightly between my thumb and forefinger, delighting in her yelp as I rolled the peak slowly.

"I think you know," I said. "The question is..." I gave a light tug to the sensitive tip and she gripped my hair at the roots, her back bowing to give me more access. "Do you want me to stop?"

When she didn't respond I threaded my hand through her hair and pulled her head back gently. I kissed down her throat and chest until I got to her clothed nipple, pulling it into my mouth for a long *suck.*

The moan that came spilling from her mouth made me shudder. I pulled away, trailing hot, open mouthed kisses to her other breast before capturing her other lightly abused nipple in my mouth.

"Will you really not take it off?" she whined, squirming.

My response was a light bite that had her clenching her thighs.

"That would be cheating," I said and let the hand that was holding her hair trail down her spine, my fingers ghosting along her smooth skin until I reached her ass. I gave it a light squeeze —the best I could, anyway, with our awkward position—before skating my fingers to her front and finding the lace of her panties once more.

I slipped my fingers into the material, playing with the edge of it. It wasn't enough to touch where I truly wanted—where Hazel was clearly growing more desperate by the minute to have me—but they did brush against the light tuft of curls hidden behind the fabric.

She put pressure on the back of my head, guiding me back

to her nipple. I obliged and pulled it into my mouth. My reward was a moan and her spreading her legs for me.

I stood, pushing the stool back with my foot as I straightened. My mouth brushed against the side of hers, not quite a kiss, but as close as I was willing to do without her prompting.

I trailed my hand slowly to cup her pussy. So slowly that she could have stopped me at any time.

But she didn't.

She didn't want me to stop.

Just that thought alone caused my entire body to fill with satisfaction. I wasn't just making it up.

She *wanted* me.

Her underwear was already slightly damp. I ran my fingers through her folds, finding her slick and needy before putting some light pressure on her clit.

The soft noises she was making excited me, but I didn't want to force her into anything. I wanted to hear her say it. If she wanted me to fuck her, I needed to hear it coming from her mouth.

"This could mean as much or as little as you want," I whispered. "If you don't want it to mean anything, I understand. Just tell me what you want. You have to *tell* me."

Chapter 9

Hazel

I licked my overly dry lips.

Was I really going to do this?

Quinn's touch was like fire where we were connected, her finger's light pressure against my clit making it hard to think straight.

But I *wanted to*. Wanted her. Wanted this.

My fingers shook with a mix of desire and anticipation, leaving her hair and stroking along the soft skin of her face and jaw.

"It doesn't mean anything," she insisted, those delicious fingers of hers circling my clit once more and turning me liquid in her arms.

"It means *everything*," I whimpered, taking a firm hold of her face and bringing her lips to mine with all the desperation that I'd felt since I saw the 'going' icon pop up beside her name on the trip invitation.

I kissed her like she was a lifeline, like I could share a year's worth of hurt and loneliness between us without words.

Quinn. I was kissing *Quinn.* With her smart mouth and her quick hands and—

I was lifted in the air, my back and under my knees supported by Quinn's strong arms as she moved us towards the sofa. She dropped me onto the buttery cushions, covering my body with hers like a blanket as she reclaimed my lips.

"I've dreamt of this," she growled, her lips trailing from mine across my cheek and to the soft spot at my jaw that always made me shudder.

"Me too," I whispered back urgently, my hands exploring the smooth expanse of her back. "Kiss, please."

Quinn's returning smile sent desire pooling at my core, the flirtatious dimple that I'd kissed a hundred times visible for a fraction of a second before her lips met mine again. I nipped at the soft flesh of her lower lip and was rewarded with a delicious groan of pleasure that I felt down to my toes.

This was really happening.

I swept my tongue over the little hurt, pausing to suck the spot gently as Quinn used her hands to part my legs further. Her fingers slipped under my panties, finding my clit for lazy circles that—after a year of near celibacy—had me quickly nearing the edge.

Our kisses were frantic, laced with the remnants of the whiskey we'd forgotten the moment the game had begun.

It hadn't been enough to get me drunk, but the liquid courage had definitely pushed me to be honest. If anything, it was Quinn I was drunk on. Her drugging kisses and excruciatingly slow circles at my cunt drawing me tight like a bow.

"Please," I whimpered.

She bit into my jaw, leaving me to feel her smile against my skin. "Please what? Tell me what you want Haze,"

"To come on your face." I gasped, my hips bucking into her

touches. "Quinn, I—oh *fuuuuck*." Whatever I was going to say next was lost as Quinn slipped two fingers inside me.

I pulled my top off, discarding it over the back of the couch with a careless toss. Quinn's eyes landed on my exposed nipples like targets.

"Haze... This is your last chance to tell me to stop. We can go to bed and forget this ever happened." Her pupils were blown with lust that I'm sure my own gaze matched, fingers pumping in and out of my core with tantalizing slowness.

"How many times do I have to tell you that I want you before you are going to hear me?" I snapped, wrapping my arms around her neck and pulling her flush against my body for a string of needy kisses. "I need you Quinn."

"Need me?" Quinn asked thickly as my hands snaked between us to play with her nipples. Her voice held that slightly teasing tone that caused my entire body to light on fire.

I nodded, letting her up just enough to bring her chest into my line of sight. My lips found her breast the moment it was exposed to me, teeth scraping against the soft flesh to her pert nipple.

Quinn let out a breathy moan as my lips closed around the tight peak, my tongue laving over the nerves. I bit down hard and she yelped, her eyes narrowing.

"Haze," her voice was a warning as she sat up, peeling my panties down to my mid thigh.

I moved to take them the rest of the way off just as Quinn gripped the lace in both hands, the telltale rip warning me that I wouldn't be wearing them again.

"I liked those," I complained half heartedly.

"I'll buy you a hundred," she swore between desperate kisses. "Whatever you want, I don't care. Now turn around."

The command in her voice was unmistakable, leaving no room for argument as I sat up and turned, stopping on my knees with my back to her front. Quinn's hands found my breasts, massaging and playing idly with the peaks as she pressed her front to my back.

She knew exactly how to tease me, but no matter how much I would complain, I loved every moment of it. And I knew that Quinn did as well. She loved the control that came with it. Loved to hear me beg for her.

"Quinn," I whined, eager to play into her desires.

She chuckled darkly in my ear, her mouth finding the crook between my shoulder and neck for a trail of nips and sucks. Shivers racked my body and I couldn't stop the whimpers falling from my mouth. Her left hand slid from where she'd been torturing my nipples, fingers brushing down my slightly rounded belly and past the small thatch of curly hair to where she could cup my pussy.

My breath caught and I pushed my hips back into her but she refused to take it any further.

"You're so impatient."

"I've waited long enough," I snapped, turning my head to capture her lips in a bruising kiss. My tongue explored her mouth as she ran her fingers through my slick folds, teasing my aching center with shallow thrusts of her fingers that had me whimpering.

She may not have forced me to beg her verbally like she once had, but she gave me no reprieve. She fucked me like she had all the time in the world and then some. Each time I felt a familiar heat rise in me and my pussy clamp around her digits, she would slow.

She smiled against my lips when I tried to ride her fingers, desperate to chase my orgasm. And when she had enough, she would use her free hand to hold me still before continuing. It was almost like a game.

One she played expertly.

I was close to begging her by the time she stopped teasing, and when she finally drove her fingers home I could have sobbed with the relief of it, Quinn's talented digits finding my g-spot and sending me hurtling towards the edge. After so many times of edging me closer and closer, the first wave of my orgasm was so powerful it caused me to stiffen against her and for the most embarrassing sounds to come from me.

"Fuck, please, don't stop Quinn—so good—I'm going to—"

I hardly knew what I was saying.

"Good girl Haze, come on my fingers. Show me how much that pretty little pussy of yours missed me."

Pleasure zipped down my spine and I moaned, burying my face into Quinn's throat. I had fantasized about being called her *good girl* once again, usually with my hand or a toy between my legs. The sounds of her praise would follow me into my dreams, where she forced me to come over and over again, begging her for release only to be rewarded with such a simple yet intoxicating praise.

"That's it," Quinn praised, scissoring her fingers slowly. "Lay on the arm of the couch, sweetheart."

I did as I was told, still half boneless from my orgasm. The position left my sopping cunt exposed to Quinn's gaze.

Somehow, in the dim light of the fire, with the subtle crackle of the wood and the warm glow washing around us, I didn't feel self conscious like I might've in the past.

Who would think that Hazel the fashionista would give up her biweekly waxing appointments? If you'd have asked me two years ago I would've said no way in hell. I would have snapped my legs closed, but instead I found myself opening them for her.

Quinn freed her fingers from me and I bounced a little on the cushions as she adjusted herself, strong arms hooked around my thighs and pulled me down onto her waiting mouth.

She licked a slow stripe from my ass to my clit, swirling her tongue over the sensitive bundle of nerves and making my legs shake.

She devoured my cunt like a starving woman presented with a five course meal. Sealing her mouth around my clit and sucking hard.

Before, Quinn'd been taking her time. Savoring the moment. Now? She was on a mission. She didn't pause to make me squirm or edge me until my mind went hazy. She knew exactly what to do to force me into my next climax. And far faster than I had expected.

Before I knew it, I was riding her face. My hand reached back to tangle in her hair, forcing her mouth closer to me as I chased my own pleasure. The groan she let out against my overly sensitive clit was the thing to push me over the edge a second time. I cried out as I fell headlong over the edge, a string of nonsensical curses and praises falling from my lips.

Quinn released my clit with a wet noise, her fingers taking its place for slow, languid strokes as she pushed herself upright. Just when I thought she'd give me a break, she crowded my back, nipping my shoulder as I whimpered and gasped.

"Quinn, please, it's too much!"

"You taste even better than I remembered," she murmured, stilling her hand. She licked a stripe up my sweaty shoulder blade, humming quietly. "Scream prettier than in my dreams too."

"Sit on my face, right fucking now," I demanded—begged—already twisting to take Quinn's place.

"You're so bossy," she teased. Her lips curved into a seductive grin, still glossy with my release and she hopped off the sofa, shedding her underwear as I got comfortable on my back. She straddled my neck with her thighs, looking down her toned body to meet my eager gaze.

I lapped at her pussy, licking and sucking desperately at her sopping core. I'd planned to go slow. To be in control. But the second that Quinn's taste hit my tongue, I was a done for, a slave to the woman who hadn't left my thoughts since our first kiss in our shared freshman dorm.

Quinn whimpered and moaned above me, practically vibrating from the effort not to buck into my mouth. I felt her strong thighs tense around my head and stopped abruptly, snapping my mouth shut and turning my face.

It was the thing I needed to pull me from my lustful craze. There was one thing I needed. She may have wanted to play her games, but I wanted to play my own just as much.

"Haze–Wha—"

I looked up at her with lust and anger burning in my gaze. "For every fucking month I had to miss you, I'm going to deny you an orgasm."

Honestly, if she pushed hard enough my resolve would have softened, but I was owed this and I couldn't think of a better way to get back at her besides turning her into a writhing, begging mess. Even the image of it in my mind was enough to send another shot of heat through my body.

"You're still mad," Quinn swallowed hard, bending so she could cup my face with her hand. "We don't have to do this if—"

"Quinn, would you just shut up for five seconds? If you can stand it, don't come until I tell you that you can, I'll forget about it. We'll be even."

She licked her lips, her thumb tracing mine. "I've never been able to—"

"Well figure it out." I grinned, and rubbed at the apex of her thighs with my fingers.

She tensed, straightening back up. "Okay," she said slowly,

voice hoarse with strain as I brought her closer and closer to ecstasy.

It made me feel powerful. The way her hips bucked and fists clenched. The sounds of her pleasure each time she was a razor's edge from tipping over into an orgasm.

Again and *again,* I brought her to the edge, listening to desperate whimpers and moans. The way she praised and cursed me in the same breath.

"Please, Haze— I can't—" Quinn's thighs were shaking violently now, her desire dripping down my wrist from where I'd long buried my fingers deep inside of her. My mouth worshiping her clit.

From the outside, it might have looked like I was in control of this situation. But I was as much a slave to Quinn's whims as she was to mine. A give and take that was older than anything else in my life.

"Haze!" She was bent now, propping herself up on the arm of the sofa like a lifeline. I was sure that when we were done there would be nail marks biting into the leather, a thought almost as exciting as what would happen when I finally agreed to let Quinn finish.

I could tell she was nearly at her limit, her moans and pleas louder with every practiced swipe of my tongue. I scissored my fingers, releasing her momentarily from my mouth.

"Quinn, baby, do you want to come?"

"Yes," she gasped, riding my fingers. "Please, Haze, I'm so sorry, I'll never ice you out like that again, I—"

"I know. I want to hear you scream my name." I sealed my mouth back over the tight bundle of nerves, sucking the way I knew she liked from years of hookups and she screamed, warm wet splashing between us as she shook and convulsed, her pussy grinding against my fingers and mouth.

I took her through the aftershocks, catching my breath a

little before guiding her gently to lay beside me on the narrow cushions.

"I didn't know you could do that," I panted, swiping a hand down my soaked face.

"Me either," she grunted, face buried in the crook of my neck.

"I love you, Quinn," I whispered, so quiet I wasn't sure she'd hear over our pounding hearts, the howling wind outside and the crackle of flames.

It didn't matter if she did. It wouldn't stop it from being true.

Warm, strong arms wrapped around my waist, paired with the smell of sandalwood soap. A familiar, barely there snore rustling the back of my hair.

I didn't dare to move. Hardly dared to breathe.

I'd had this dream before. The moment I opened my eyes it would be over, and I'd realize I was alone again. Doomed to jump from place to place so I wouldn't have to deal with the ghosts haunting my brownstone. Fuck, I was practically one of them at this point.

Even if it was a lie—a dream concocted by my subconscious —I'd do anything to hold on for just a few more minutes.

Because when I got up I'd have to face my friends again. Pretend with Quinn and everyone else at the cabin that I wasn't heartbroken over the wrong person, like I was okay with Quinn and I being closer to strangers than friends.

"Are you even breathing, Haze?" Quinn murmured sleepily in my ear, her lips grazing the sensitive shell.

Hot, wet tears welled in my eyes. I'd almost forgotten the sound of her voice, it'd been so long since we'd been alone like this. But thanks to a couple days of hanging out, there it was, a perfect recreation.

My subconscious was one mean bitch.

"Haze?" Quinn asked, the cushions jostling as she sat up, her breath ghosting over my face from where the figment leaned over me. I could practically see it through my eyelids, the way her dark t-shirt would cling to her shoulders but gape at the neck, the slight frizziness to her golden hair in the morning light.

Her calloused, warm fingers brushed my cheek and I whimpered.

"This is such bullshit," I hissed to my dream.

"Babe, what?" She breathed a laugh. "Are you okay?"

I sighed, steeling myself for the inevitable disappointment of waking up alone *again*. Because if I let this go on any longer I was going to have to brave the undoubtedly cold shower for a place to cry. With that depressing thought, I opened my eyes.

Quinn's face hovered above mine, confusion pulling her brows together. "You good?"

I blinked stupidly, taking in the hickeys decorating her neck and chest. The blanket we'd been sharing pooled at her hips, revealing her deliciously tattooed skin and bare breasts, her nipples peaked in the chill of the morning.

The fire must've guttered out overnight.

"I—" I started, breaking off into an unexpected sob as the night flooded back.

The argument. The game. *Us.*

I pulled Quinn down on top of me, burying my face into the side of her neck as I cried. Not cute girlish tears—*wailing*—snotty and uncontrollable as I caught up to a year of desperately missing her and the insurmountable joy of having her back.

Quinn was frozen for a moment before her hands began to

soothe at anywhere she could reach. "It's okay, Haze. It doesn't have to mean anything."

I hiccuped and sobbed harder at her misreading the situation.

Didn't she get it? Didn't she understand that I loved her? Wanted her? Chased after her for months in a desperate attempt to get her back after fucking up any chance we had at being anything after the funeral?

"You're so stupid!" I shouted in between gasps.

"I know," she muttered wryly. "Want to tell me why?"

I sniffed loudly, rubbing my gross, tear soaked, snotty face into the side of her marked up neck. "How can you say it means nothing? You're everything to me Quinn. I've been trying to fucking tell you that since last year."

"I'm not sure if you're being more cute or more gross right now," Quinn muttered, rolling us so she could soothe her hand down my back.

"Both, probably." I sniffed again and pulled away enough to meet her troubled blue gaze.

"Are you good?"

"Maybe," I conceded with another sniff.

"Good, then c'mere." Quinn tugged me against her chest, her lips finding the top of my head. "I'm not going anywhere, at least not until I am dressed enough to dri—ouch!"

I'd pinched her hard on the side of the boob, scowling. "Not funny."

"Don't worry Haze," she chuckled. "I'm not going anywhere."

I shivered, pulling the blanket tighter around us. "Okay."

She tilted my face towards hers, her thumb and forefinger resting on my chin. "Good morning, by the way."

"Morning," I replied, a little embarrassed as my tears started to dry in salted streaks down my cheeks.

Quinn leaned forward, kissing me in slow passes of our mouths. Her lips wrapped around mine like she'd memorized them. For all I knew, she had. Want ignited in my belly, but I made no move to take things further, content to kiss and explore, to re-familiarize myself with her wicked mouth.

Besides, we had nothing but time.

Chapter 10

Quinn

I rubbed my gloveless hands, bringing them to my mouth for a huff of hot air.

The morning air was so crisp it almost burned as it went down. Nothing like what I got in the city; it wasn't until I was faced with the freezing cold of the morning—undampened by the millions of bodies and cars of Brooklyn—that I began to miss the smog of the city.

I let out a sigh as I fell to my knees in the snow.

Today's mission: find some firewood.

As much as I loved using the cold as an excuse to cuddle with Hazel, we needed the warmth. It'd taken me way too long to pull myself off the couch bed, but I let myself have the moment. After all, I had no idea when or if I would be able to cuddle with Hazel ever again. Or feel her body against mine—taste her lips as her eyes still squinted with sleep.

But reality was calling, and as much as I wanted to stay wrapped in her arms forever, letting Hazel become a popsicle wasn't on the top of my to do list. So, we were forced out into the snow. Over two feet had fallen overnight, leaving every branch and twig around the cabin too wet to throw in the fire with any real success.

Which meant here I was, on my knees with wetness from the snow seeping into my pants as I hunted under the wrap-around porch for anything we could use to keep warm.

Hazel's flustered, tear-soaked expression flashed through my mind, making me grumble under my breath.

The things I do for her.

The only place to check was under the back deck and I prayed to whatever god was out there that there *was* some firewood down there. Otherwise we were totally screwed.

A treacherous little tug in my mind warned that if there was no fire, we'd have to be naked to keep warm. Which meant that I could explore Hazel's body with the cover of our survival.

It was dark under the deck but I could *just* make out some stray branches, decaying leaves, and litter. With hands shaking from the cold, I reached under and pulled out everything I could reach, straining my arm to get even the smallest of twigs. Since my fingers were already numb, it was hard to tell exactly how dry they were but when I pulled them out, they looked promising.

"Haze!" I yelled behind me. "I think I found some!"

I heard her footsteps crunching through the snow behind me and motioned for her to come without looking at her. Her silence should have been a warning that something was up, but I was blissfully unaware of her plans as I considered wriggling under the deck to search for more.

"I think there is more under here. I'm not sure I can fit any further in. If you don't mind crawling a bit I bet we'd have enough—"

I saw the flash of white in my peripheral vision before I felt the ice cold snow hit me right in the side of the face. The shock of the coldness was enough to stun me for a moment but as soon as I heard Hazel's crazed giggle I pushed myself up, discarding the branches onto the deck and darting towards her.

I caught a quick look at her expression. It was one that threatened to knock the breath out of my lungs while simultaneously breaking my heart in half.

Her eyes were wide and filled with a light I hadn't seen in her for ages. Perfect, pouty, pink lips pulled into a big smile—a *real* one. It was like I was seeing her again for the first time.

My Haze.

I couldn't help but let out a laugh of my own as she shrieked and ran in the opposite direction, dark hair streaming behind her. I leaned down to grab a handful of snow and began shaping it.

"You're in for it!"

She turned, realizing I wasn't following her anymore, giving me the perfect shot at her face.

But, of course, being the gentlelady I was, I would *never* hit a girl in her face.

She cursed as the snowball hit her square in the chest. Her arms flailing outward, put off balance from the impact—before she could steady herself, she fell straight back into a snow drift.

I couldn't hold in my laughter as I stalked towards her, my face muscles aching from disuse. She hadn't moved an inch as she laid there in the snow. the cutest angry expression on her face as she stared up at me. Her face was red from being out in the snow for the last few hours, a hat pulled on tight over her ears. With a little coaxing I'd gotten her into her thickest pants, boots, and of course *my gloves* before we left this morning.

"You're an asshole, you know that?" she grumbled.

Just a few days ago I would have sold my kidney to see Hazel like this again. It was hard to believe how quickly things changed between us. Faster and with more ferocity than a winter storm.

I held out my hand and she pouted, looking the other way.

With an exaggerated sigh I bent to my knees and leaned over her, she refused to look at me even as I moved to be within her eyesight.

"Don't get grumpy because you lost at your own game," I teased, a light smirk spreading across my face.

Her eyes met mine and she gave me a smile—my breath caught, warmth spreading into my chest—just as she slammed a handful of icy slush right into my face. I jerked back, trying to wipe it away but she was there in a flash, straddling me and pushing my back into the snow.

Whatever boundaries we'd before this trip had evaporated, all the tension lost between us as she leaned in. I captured her lips with mine, my freezing hands pushing themselves behind her coat to gather warmth from the skin of her back.

She let out a whine at the coldness of them, but I didn't stop kissing her. I couldn't. Whatever control I had held onto was gone, snapped like a rubber band pulled too tight.

Chris' memory was in the back of my mind, threatening me with the guilt of what we were doing ... but kissing Hazel made all the voices telling me this was wrong all but a whisper.

She bit my lip as I undid her bra with one hand. When I slipped my hands between her bra and played with her nipples, she pulled away from me entirely.

"As much as I want to cross fucking Quinn in the snow off my bucket list," she said with a breathless grin. "I think I would enjoy this much more with a fire going."

I nodded, unable to speak round the sudden lump in my throat.

The guilt was coming back full force. It happened like this every time. I'd lose myself in her, forget about everything else in the world, and then as soon as reality came crashing back so did the guilt.

She helped me up and I collected an armful of the firewood before we slowly started our way back to the house, our shoulders brushing like our bodies were magnets drawn together by some other force. I made a point of grabbing her gloved hand and she shot me a smile before looking back out behind us.

The cabins in this area were spread so far apart that there probably wasn't another living soul within at least half a mile. It was quiet. *Serene.*

Hazel looked at peace with a small smile on her face. I let her take her time on the way back, even though the bundle in my arms was a bit heavy. She could take a look at the scenery as if cataloging the entire place ... and I would watch her.

It'd been a while since I had wanted to draw someone, but I had an overwhelming urge to draw her now. The morning sun hit her face so perfectly, and with the white snow as a backdrop, she looked angelic.

A cold and shivering one, but an angel nonetheless.

We thumped up the steps, Hazel letting out a grateful groan as she threw the door open and was met with a gust of warm air.

The first thing I noticed was the sound of the tv going, then that all the lights were back on.

Hazel and I met each other's gazes with matching expressions of excitement and shock.

"The power is back on," she breathed.

I closed and locked the door behind us and threw the branches onto the floor, prowling towards Hazel slowly. She grinned as I grabbed her by the back of her thighs, hiking them around my waist.

"I have an idea on what we can do to celebrate," I murmured against her lips.

Her giggle followed us up the stairs and into the bathroom.

I didn't have to tell her to remove her clothes, she was

already shedding them as I walked. She hissed as the warmth of her jacket fell away, pulling away a moment to tug off her sweater. The removal of her shirt caused me to lose balance, but her lips were back on mine in seconds, soft yet demanding. I reached blindly with one hand down the hall, trying to keep an eye on where we were going, but as soon as we reached the bathroom I plopped her ass on the counter and turned to start the shower, putting it on its hottest setting.

By the time I returned she'd already discarded her pants and gave me a sly grin. I pushed the door closed and walked straight between the silent invitation of her open legs.

I took my time gathering her hair, combing my hand through the silky strands, enjoying the look she gave me and the way she leaned into whichever hand was running through her hair. I placed chaste kisses on her mouth and trailed them down to her throat. I wasn't going to be rushed today. Not when we were alone. Not while the steam from the shower began to fog the mirror beyond her shoulder, obscuring the reverent look in my reflection's eyes.

I was gentle in the way I handled her, wanting to savor every whimper and moan she gifted my ears. When I got all of her hair in one hand I tugged on the makeshift ponytail, forcing her to bare her neck to me.

I licked and sucked the column of her neck, teeth grazing over the sensitive skin. I was tempted to mark her, whether it be with my teeth or a hickey, but stopped before I could do something we could regret. We may be wearing winter clothes, but there was no doubt the others would see my marks eventually. And a part of me didn't mind so much that Hazel's love was littered across my skin, but I wouldn't put her in the same position. Though was positive that when they saw the marks, their questions would be relentless.

Still, I allowed myself to nibble on the sensitive flesh and was rewarded with a gasp. It only caused the desire that I felt for her to burn hotter; the small sounds she made were enough to drive me to insanity with need

For *her*.

Hazel worked to undo my pants while I kissed down to her chest. She arched into me, leaving me no choice but to take one of her erect nipples into my mouth. I couldn't help but watch as she leaned her head back against the mirror that was slowly starting to fog with a hiss at the cold glass.

I'd always been enamored by Hazel. Whether it was the way she took her life into her own hands, or the way she looked as she came around my fingers. Everything she did was so awe-inspiring I wasn't surprised to feel the warmth in my chest that I associated with our relationship so long ago.

Obsessed. I have and always will be obsessed with her.

It had always been that way. She was always special to me. She had always been the one I felt the most at peace with and my world had changed drastically so that she was in the center of it.

In my heart I knew the word, but I couldn't bear to say it. Let alone think it.

I'd given up my claim. Pushed her into the arms of someone else.

When she successfully undid my pants and forced her hand into my underwear, I did the same to her. I didn't remove my gaze, or stop sucking and biting her nipple as I circled her clit.

Her own hand copied my movements and I let out a low moan. I leaned into her, trailing kisses back up to neck before pushing two fingers into her.

I'd hardly touched her, hardly had the chance to tease, and she was so slick that I found no resistance as I stroked the walls of her slick cunt. It made my pussy clench with a need of my own.

From her position, it would have been awkward to try the same so she continued to circle my clit. I brought my hand to her back and pushed her closer to the edge so I could better fuck her.

I pulled away so I could watch her, determined to memorize every tiny change in her face—every little change between us. I didn't know how long I could pretend that she was mine, but I was sure as hell going to take advantage of it.

Her eyes snapped open when I ground the heel of my palm against her clit, the knuckles of her free hand white on the countertop.

She was splayed in front of me, naked with her leg spread to offer me space between her thighs. My mouth hooked into a rare smirk as I trailed my eyes down her flushed body to where her pretty little pussy swallowed my fingers. She followed my gaze, the image of my fingers disappearing inside her only to reappear dripping with her desire so erotic that she clenched around my fingers. The chorus of her accompanying pants and whines making my pussy throb.

For a moment, she was *mine.*

Spread open for *me.* Wet for *me.*

Her eyes begging for *me* to fuck her like I meant it.

"Quinn," she breathed, hardly audible over the water rushing to meet the tiles of the shower. "*More.*"

I slowed my thrusts, making sure to grind my palm into the sensitive bundle of nerves every time I sunk into her. She'd forgotten about my own aching clit and brought her still wet hand to wrap around my wrist, urging me futilely faster.

But I wouldn't be rushed, not while I had her in my grip.

I leaned in close, just enough to brush my lips across hers. Hazel leaned forward instantly and I pulled away, denying her the kiss she so clearly wanted as my hand on her back moved to her throat.

I would *dominate* this woman. *Possess* her. Remind her which of us was in control.

"Fuck, you're so wet," I murmured, my thumb brushing her jaw. "You've been waiting for this all morning haven't you?"

She let out an almost pained whimper as I slowed my pace.

"I love seeing you like this," I said, putting light pressure on her throat with a squeeze of my inked fingers. "Naked— writhing and begging for more. Promise that this is for me. Promise me that you'll *only* be like this for me. Then, maybe if you beg *properly,* I'll let you come."

When she didn't respond I began to slowly circle her clit with my thumb. It was enough pressure for her to jerk in my hold, but not enough to send her hurtling towards her orgasm like her moans desperately told me she wanted.

"Quinn, *please.*" Her voice was strained, her hand gripped my wrist and tried to force me to move faster, *harder.* But I was the one in control here and I wanted—no—*needed* to hear her say it.

"Say it, Haze," I whispered. "Tell me that your wet pussy is *all* mine."

Selfish, selfish thoughts.

She jerked forward when I curled my finger inside of her and let out a breathy moan.

"Tell me that you belong to me."

"Fuck, Quinn," she ground out, her nails digging into the sensitive skin of my wrist. "Fine. It's yours—I'm yours—Now *please,* fuck me properly!"

"Good girl," I purred.

I leaned forward and swiped my tongue across her lips. When she opened her mouth to deepen the kiss, I squeezed her throat lightly as a reminder.

"I don't need to teach you how to beg properly do I?" I asked with a raised brow.

Hazel's reaction was immediate, a glare that transformed her desperate features—however briefly—into the brat I knew she was. Unfortunately for her, I'd had a long, long year of thinking of the ways I would fuck the attitude right out of her.

"Say, '*Quinn, my wet,* needy *cunt is all yours*'." I didn't bother to hide my smile; egging her on was just too delicious.

Her eyes trailed to my mouth, the pause between us lasting long enough I thought she'd outright refuse.

"My wet..." I scissored my fingers inside her and she inhaled sharply. "*Needy* cunt..." I rewarded her obedience with the curl of my fingers into the sensitive spot she liked best, reveling in the reward of the way her thighs shook. "Is all *yours!*"

"Beg me," I commanded, licking my lips. My mouth had gone dry at the display, my breathing shallow pants. "Beg me to make you come."

Hazel wrapped her hand around my wrist, the green of her eyes nearly lost to her blown pupils. "Quinn, *please.* I need you," she gasped. "*Please.*"

I began to fuck her harder then, thrusting my fingers in and out of her so hard the sounds of them inside her wet cunt becoming louder than the shower behind us. Her head dropped back and a low curse slipped from her lips.

"Ah—*fuck,*" she moaned. "Just like that Qui—nnh—oh fuck—"

I paused and she let out a whine of protest.

"Beg," I reminded.

"Please Quinn," she begged, breathless. "Please fuck me until I'm coming so hard on your fingers that my scream echoes through the house. So hard that I will feel you days after. Make me come so hard that there will never be *anyone* that tops—"

I didn't let her finish, diving forward to capture her lips with mine. It wasn't long until she was coming around me, but I wouldn't stop at a single orgasm.

No, I needed *more*.

She slumped back against the mirror as I pulled away.

I didn't make her beg anymore, content to take my time as I was reacquainted with her familiar desires. After the first orgasm I was gentler, sweeter. It wasn't about me owning her anymore, it was about her owning me. A love letter written with my hands and mouth on her skin.

This was different than last night. Different from the majority of times we fucked, actually.

We had a bad habit of getting so wound up that we'd shred each others clothes in the rush to touch, to taste, to *fuck*. Get so lost in our pleasure that we'd go until one of us couldn't move.

This was ... intimate in a way we never were before. Slow.

I didn't rush and she didn't push me to.

I took my time exploring her like I should've on those stupid twin sized beds in our dorm. Watched how she reacted as I curled my fingers inside her. The way her lips trembled when I used my other hand to circle her clit. The flash of a shiver as I pushed another finger into her, stretching her opening to accommodate the additional intrusion.

My name fell from her lips more times than I could count. It made my chest ache.

I couldn't handle this. It was one thing to fuck each other, but what we were doing now was so much more than that. It came with strings. Hangups. *Guilt*.

Acting like she was mine, as if we were the only two people in this world. As if her fiancé hadn't just died. It was cruel. A sick fantasy that I'd stumbled into like a snowdrift.

Hazel came again, her praises and moans high and bright against the tiles. I watched it as if it was the last time, greedily taking her in and picking up the movement on her clit, wanting to ride it out as long as possible.

When she finally came down, a wicked smile curved her beautiful, kiss swollen mouth. She reached out to me, aiming to pick up where she left off but I grabbed her hand.

If I let her touch me, I'd never be able to walk away from her again. I needed to keep a clear head. This was over the second we left the bathroom. It had to be.

The steam from the shower was getting overwhelming—a perfect excuse.

"Come on, Haze," I said in a soft tone as I helped her off the counter. "Let's shower and then I promise to make you a delicious breakfast."

She laughed softly and shook her head, letting me pull her into the stall. "Whatever you want Quinn."

"Soup and hot chocolate," Hazel said dryly. "A delicious breakfast indeed."

I looked at her sidelong, settling into the stool beside her with a small smile.

It would be so easy to pull her in between my legs to hold her like I did this morning, but I held myself back. I couldn't keep acting like things were good between us when I knew that I'd lied to her for the last two years.

"I'd like to see you do better," I teased.

She flipped me off before digging into her soup, a stupid smile curling the corners of her mouth.

In the time we'd spent confined together in the cabin, the light started to slowly return to her eyes. Like the sun peeking through the clouds after a particularly heavy rainstorm—you could almost see the darkness hanging over her when I'd arrived at Stargazer's Lake. And yet, here she was now, practically glowing.

I knew realistically that it would never go away, forever. But the pressure of worry in my chest lessened as I realized the small change.

Nothing good came without a cost. And it was something we'd both pay for dearly.

"I'll have you know I am a great cook."

I rolled my eyes. I didn't remember her being a good cook when we were in school. I *did* remember her almost burning down the shared common space because of a grease fire *multiple* times though. She didn't improve when she and Chris bought the loft either.

"And exactly how many weeks of clean up duty did you have to serve after getting the fire department called to our dorm?" I asked with a raised brow.

After the firefighters left the head RA had thought it would be a fitting punishment that Hazel cleaned up her own mess. She'd tried to get away with pushing it off for *days* until the RA got fed up and locked her out of her dorm until it was finished.

She sent me a burning look, the familiar argument dragging with it familiar feelings.

"You know that wasn't my fault," she insisted, pushing her soup towards me.

I waved her off and motioned for her to eat it first. I didn't want to tell her that we were seriously running low on supplies. She was already too skinny as it was—and it wasn't me who got an attitude when she was hungry.

Power or no power, if we had no food, we were screwed and I wanted to make sure she was taken care of.

"Yes, I guess the pouring hot grease into a wet sink was the doing of a ghost," I muttered.

She sat up straight, her cheeks puffing.

"Okay it was my fault! But I did get better! I literally spent an entire *year* in a cooking class after I almost ruined Chris's favorite pan—" She cut herself off before I could, realization of what she said written all over her face.

Her eyes searched my face for a tense moment before she stared straight down at the bowl.

The comfortable teasing between us evaporated, leaving behind an uncomfortable silence that let my guilt fester.

Chris, the dead fiancé. My best fucking friend. The guy I was totally screwing over by moving in on his girl. The girl I pushed him towards.

The entire reason we were even here to begin with. My best friend ... or *was*.

It was kinda hard to call him a friend at all when he not only tried to marry the only woman I ever saw a future with, and then forced me to keep his fucking secrets for him. Secrets that would threaten to rip my chest apart for *months*—and ruin even my *friendship* with Hazel.

For a while I pretended that I was happy for them—I did set them up after all, so I clearly thought it was a good idea at some point—but after I got my head out of my ass and realized what I wanted. *Who* I wanted, it'd been too late.

I was the reason Hazel and I—you couldn't call it a break up, but to call it just fucking seemed a little oversimplified—in the first place. We told everyone it was mutual, but it was obvious to anyone with eyes that I was the one that pushed her away.

Years after we graduated, I started to realize that I was wrong about *everything*. A part of me thought I was being noble, that I was saving Hazel from a boring and completely unsatisfactory life. But it was just my cowardly way of pushing her away.

It didn't help that I only realized it after she had gotten

with someone so much better for her than I was and I was stuck as a third wheel between the two because there was no way I would ruin their chance at true happiness.

I swallowed thickly and looked towards my hot chocolate. I knew the right thing to do would be to talk about him. It helps with the grief. We *should* be sharing the memories we had of him and remembering how he was when he was alive—instead of moping that he was gone.

But I didn't have anything nice to say about Chris, not now. All I could think about was his stupid, demanding voice on the other line of the phone and how he'd forced me and everyone else to make a decision that could affect Hazel's life.

I thought if I stayed away, I'd be able to handle the weight of our secret ... but every moment I spent alone with her, *pretending* as if she was mine, it was too much.

What were supposed to be moments between us that I'd only dreamed of turned sour because all I could think about was how we had to watch Hazel continue to fall in love with Chris when he *knew* he was dying.

Fucking prick.

I cleared my throat and shifted in my seat, leaning my chin on my hand. "Didn't he get them imported or something?" I asked, fighting to keep my tone light. "That's an expensive thing to ruin."

I only knew because I'd actually tried to buy him one for Christmas. I saw how much he liked his cookware and thought it would be a nice gesture. After he told me the brand though, I settled for something half the price. Turns out that a tattoo artist from Brooklyn's salary couldn't compete with a trust fund baby.

Her eyes lingered on me for a moment before looking back down at the soup. Slowly, a smile spread across her face.

"I said *almost*," she muttered. "I stood there for hours trying to buff the marks out but it only made things worse. You know the worst part?"

I had an inkling. "He wasn't even mad?"

She shook her head and let out a laugh.

"I started bawling the moment he walked into the door and all he did was pull me into a hug and say he could buy another," she scoffed. "I spent three hours buffing the damn thing and the rich asshole barely even looked at it."

She crossed her arms over her chest in a sort of self hug, a far off look in her eyes. But it wasn't pain she was lost of this time; instead her features were serene, like the memory was fond.

"I miss him," I admitted. I wasn't sure where the need to suddenly confess to her was, but I couldn't stop myself. "Obviously there were things that we disagreed on—"

"Literally everything?" she asked with a teasing smile.

Like pineapple on pizza, baseball teams, what counted as real music, pancakes vs waffles ... you.

If I had a choice, I would've never kept his diagnosis from her. I would have gone home, told her right away, instead of having everyone in her life *lie* to her.

"You could say that," I murmured, using my hot chocolate as an excuse to avoid her eyes. Anything I could do to push past the unbearable feeling of guilt welling up inside me.

Chapter 11

Hazel

"I s it weird, talking about him?" I asked, using my pinky to stir my hot chocolate. The little marshmallows had long since dissolved, leaving a foamy top that was perfectly sweet.

It was a little weird to me, if I was being honest, but I didn't want to constantly go over what happened. He died, we lived; nothing was going to change that and I shouldn't let it control my life any more than it had already.

"Kind of," Quinn said, shifting in her seat.

It didn't escape my notice that, since our shower, she hadn't made a move to touch me. I tried not to let it hurt my feelings, but maybe I misread the situation—maybe Quinn was still *Quinn* and I was good enough to fuck, but not anything else.

I had been so lost in everything else for the last few months that I forgot what even led me to be with Chris in the first place.

"I think it's more that part of me doesn't know how he'd feel about—"

"Us?" I interrupted, cringing at the hopefulness in my

voice. I didn't want to hear what Quinn would call it, especially since she was likely to say 'our hookup'.

"Yeah, *us*," she replied with a faint tilt of her lips, watching with rapt attention as I sucked the hot chocolate and melted marshmallow off my finger.

The little quirk of her lips caused a shot of hope to light my chest, but I quickly pushed it down. She may not have brushed it off as an unimportant hookup, but it still wasn't everything I wanted.

A part of me had wished that she had changed the last few years and had finally been looking for something more serious ... but maybe it was because it was *me*. Maybe I was the problem and not Quinn's flakiness.

"I feel like he'd probably be happy about it. It's not like we ever lied to him—he knew we had history. Not to mention was your best friend through most of it—Maybe not hooking up at his funeral *but* I did warn you that if I drank all of that whiskey you were in for a bad time.'

"I didn't have a bad time," Quinn protested, grabbing my hand and pulling it towards her over the countertop. "What made you think I had a bad time?"

"You didn't call me for a year, that's what."

"You needed space so you could grieve."

"Space?" I laughed unkindly, shaking my head. "That's what you want to call freezing me out for a year?'

At first, I'd called and texted so much that it was legitimately embarrassing to think about. But after two weeks of absolutely *nothing*, I took the hint and cut my losses. Sure, I cried for like three days after she didn't call me on my birthday. Or our friendaversary. But I ... I was over it now.

Totally over it.

"I thought, with time ... it would get easier."

I scoffed and folded my arms. "How about next time you

listen to what I want instead of being a mega-asslord-mc-douche-face? I know you were thinking about me anyway—I can see when you watch my Instagram story, you know."

The color left Quinn's face. "What?"

"Didn't you know that?"

"I—well—"

I rolled my eyes. "If you texted me half the times that you thought about me, it wouldn't have to be like this."

"I couldn't."

Anger boiled in my veins. *She couldn't?* More like she had never wanted to in the first place.

"What do you mean you *couldn't?*" I snapped, my frustration returning full force. "I thought you were giving me space or some bullshit I didn't ask for! You want me to believe that it was some huge sacrifice on your part? As if you weren't making the rounds through the panties of every girl you—"

"Hazel," Quinn cut off my rapidly rising voice with her own, quiet and intense. She stood from her stool and crowded into my personal space, long fingers cupping around the back of my neck and jaw. "There was *never* anyone else. There has never been anyone else. There never will be anyone else for me, but *you.*"

I opened and closed my mouth several times, eyes wide with shock. "What are you saying?"

"I'm saying that, for me, there has only ever been you. I have loved you ever since I laid eyes on you. Loved you enough that when I realized I couldn't give you what you needed that I let you find someone—*my best fucking friend, mind you*—to be that for you."

Her hands felt like fire where she touched me, burning me down to my core with the desperate longing I'd felt in her absence.

She'd been the one to walk away from me. The one to turn me down. Not the other way around.

My mind was whirling. Every moment I had with her, even when I was still with Chris, flashed across my mind. *Even then? Even as she watched me fall in love with him? Plan to marry him?*

"You—But—*Still?*"

"Of course, still!" She laughed, resting her forehead against mine. "It killed me to be apart from you, Haze. At least when you were with Chris, I was still in your life. I've watched it all, sweetheart, every story, every post, every vlog—*everything*. It's all nothing—pointless—in comparison to the real thing."

"You could've just picked up the phone," I insisted. My hand was wrapped so tightly in her shirt my knuckles were white. I couldn't even remember when I'd reached out and grabbed it.

"You needed time. Fuck, you probably needed time since we found out last April but I—"

"What do you mean, April?" I asked, my blood going cold. "What did I find out in April?"

Chapter 12

Quinn

L ie.
>   *Brush it off. Create some stupid story.*
>   *Just fucking lie, Quinn.*

But I couldn't. I couldn't keep lying anymore. Not to her. Not when the burden of bearing Chris' secrets had single handedly crushed the relationship Hazel and I had.

Or the one we could have had.

I wanted to stay in this bubble of warmth for a lifetime. I wanted to tell her over and over again how I had loved her since the moment I saw her.

How dare *she think that I had a bad time and that's why I didn't call?*

It was because I couldn't stomach looking at her afterwards. She had been so distraught by the sudden decline in his health and subsequent death and seeing her at his funeral only made me feel worse about keeping a dead man's secret. About putting Chris and his fucking pride over Hazel's feelings.

I thought I was doing something for the both of them, but

in the end all I did was hurt Hazel and make things impossible for me.

"I—Listen—Before I tell you, I need you to know that all we ever wanted was the best for you." My voice was a shaky whisper, hardly more than a breath. Like I could somehow keep her from being angry by being sorry.

The humor had left her face and she was staring at me with a mix of fear and anger. Inside, I think she knew what I was about to say. *She had to, right?*

"Quinn," she warned, the playful teasing was gone from her voice now. Replaced with icy fury

I reached for the hand that she'd tangled in my shirt, but she snapped it away. Even though I knew I deserved it, the action still hurt.

"Hazel—You gotta understand. Both of you were our—"

"Cut to the point," she demanded, her voice turning hard.

I swallowed thickly.

"The April before he died, Chris called me," I said.

Her eyes widened and I couldn't look at them any more. My eyes fell to my hands, my fingernail digging at my cuticle. "He told me about his diagnosis. That it was terminal. He asked that we—"

"You knew since *April?*" Hazel breathed in a mixture of horror and outrage.

It was like all the anger had rushed out of her in that one sentence and she was left with barely enough strength to utter the words.

I nodded.

"And *you* didn't tell me?" The hurt had seeped into her voice and felt like a slap. "What about being the girl you *loved,* huh?" She spit the word like a curse. "How could you have kept something like this from me? I only had a few—"

Her voice cracked, making me look up at her.

Immediately, I wished I didn't.

Her eyes were red and glassy with tears, a few already tracking down her face.

"It was his last wish," I reasoned, the words bitter in my mouth. "How was I supposed to deny my best friend his last wish?"

Then she really started to cry, her hands balled into fists at her side. I reached out to bring her to me, but she pushed me away with enough force that I almost fell backward.

"How many people knew?" she choked out.

I couldn't answer her.

'Everyone except you' sounded too harsh.

But she got the message loud and clear anyway.

"Fucking *bastards*," she muttered under her breath, running a hand through her hair. "I can't believe all of you watched while I fell further and further in love with him— knowing damn fucking well that he'd be dead in a few months."

"We wanted you to be happy, Haze," I said and reached my hand out for her. "You would have spent the last few months looking at him like he was already gone. He wanted to live his life with you—Have fun. He didn't want you to suffer with him."

Hazel let out a bitter laugh.

"Selfish, all of you are so fucking *selfish*," she said. "How could you think that this was out of love? If this happened to you, I would make sure you knew. I wouldn't *dare* keep you in the dark."

I tried to take a step closer but she backed away. Her hand flew out to motion for me to stop.

"Please Haze—"

"No, Quinn!" She shouted, looking at me for the first time. "Fuck you, fuck you to the moon and back—not only did you lie to me, which on its own is just incredibly messed up. But then, to help you with your own fucking guilt you left me to hang for a fucking year."

"Hazel—"

"You punished me for keeping Chris' secret. And you know what? Good for you! Let me tell you a secret Quinn—" Hazel stood up on tiptoe, her face so close to mine that in a different circumstance we would've been kissing. "You are the most painfully selfish fuck boy I have ever met, and if I ever have to look at you again it'll be too fucking soon."

I was frozen. Rooted to the spot. Hazel had every right to be angry with me, to be angry with all of us. But I'd forgotten in the last year one crucial thing about Hazel Kirby—she was the only person in my entire, miserable life who saw me for exactly what I was and loved me anyway.

And she saw right fucking through me. She had somehow picked up every single degrading thought I had about myself and spat them right back at me.

"I'm going to be sick," she snapped, turning to leave.

My hand snapped out before I could think, winding around her wrist to pull her back. There's no way I was going to let her walk off on me again, not with everything out on the table. This was my opportunity to finally lay it all out for her—but just as I was about to open my mouth to do so, the sound of the door being all but kicked open rang throughout the silence.

"We're back, love birds! Make yourself presentable!" Matt yelled, his booming voice bouncing off the walls only moments before his smiling face came into view. His eyes jumped back and forth between us before the smile slowly slid off his face.

Alex was next, his normally stoic expression twisting as he took in Hazel's tear-filled eyes and the furious curl of her lip.

Matt let out a forced laugh.

"Quinnie, you were supposed to comfort her," he joked awkwardly. "Not make her cry."

Max appeared to the side of Alex, looking at the brunette with a question in her eyes.

Matt bounded forward, reaching out to pull Hazel into a hug but she smacked his hand away.

"Don't," she murmured, her voice was grief-stricken and hit me straight in my heart. She backed away from all of us with an expression that reminded me a bit of the time that a squirrel was trapped in the cabin. Like she was looking for an exit or was about to bite.

Matt's face morphed into one of pure shock, his eyes snapping to me. "Quinn–"

"I'm sorry," I whispered, looking back at Hazel. "I'm so sorry."

"You didn't," Lexie said, appearing in the doorway with a bag full of groceries.

The realization of what just happened seemed to dawn on the group and everyone moved to speak at the same time.

"He made me promise–"

"Hazel you gotta know–"

"Chris is a fucking asshole—"

"Please just let me explain–"

Hazel wasn't having any of it.

"Stop!" Her voice was hoarse, pained.

My eyes started to burn, my throat closing with the promise of tears. I looked up to the ceiling and blinked rapidly, unwilling to let the weak, pitiful part of me claim some kind of empathy.

"How dare you all keep this from me. How the fuck do you call yourselves my friends?" The shuffling of her feet against the hardwood snapped my gaze to her. She pushed past the group—headed straight towards her purse, still sitting near the entrance of the cabin.

"Haze," I whispered. My voice was pathetic to my own ears.

She shot me a tearful glower that made my heart clench.

"Enough out of you," she hissed. "You're the worst of them."

She cast a last glance at the group, shook her head, and grabbed the closest coat on the rack—the second closest actually, because she visibly recoiled when her fingers touched mine.

"Let's just talk about this Hazel," Lexie begged, dropping the groceries and slowly inching towards her.

Acting like Hazel was a frightened dog and it only made everything *so much worse.*

Hazel wasn't scared, she was *angry.*

I'd seen Hazel go through a lot.

Heartbreak, family deaths, when they took her favorite drinks off the coffee shop menu right before finals, but she'd never been one to get angry. At least not like this. It was easy to get under her skin, but this kind of anger hadn't been something I'd ever experienced from her.

Not even when I blew her off to go out with Jenna Carmichael—a date I quite literally didn't even show up for. I sat in my car in an Olive Garden parking lot for six hours before I finally gave up and went home.

But ask the girl I actually liked on a date? Get fucked college Quinn.

I didn't know what to do, and by the looks of everyone's faces, they didn't know what to do either. They hadn't expected me to spill this secret, but more importantly no one expected her to react like *this.*

I was pretty sure that Hazel didn't have the capacity to hate anyone, or anything. But I was wrong. She definitely could.

Me.

"There is nothing to say," Hazel spat. "You all made that very fucking clear."

No one moved to stop her as she left.

The door slammed so hard it made the glittering ornaments on the tree shiver. Silence fell over the room, no one daring to move. Then, as if on queue, every single head turned toward me.

The silence was deafening, four expressions of anger, disgust, and sadness staring back at me.

Alex found his voice first. "Quinn you idiot" He took off his glasses and pinched the bridge of his nose. Frustration poured off him in waves, Max and Matt close by with twin expressions of frustration. "What the fuck did you do?" His question was rhetorical, we all knew what happened.

I'd really fucked up.

Chapter 13

Hazel

I pressed the red 'ignore call' button for what felt like the thousandth time since I'd left the cabin. It was New Years Eve Eve and I was due for traditional drinks at Garrison—this shitty pub we found in college that we all still frequented despite graduating three years ago—*with all of my 'friends'*.

But I wouldn't be attending.

Fuck no I wouldn't.

Was I over Chris' death? As much as a girl could be over her fiancé dying unexpectedly of a disease that he pretended not to know about until we were in the hospital and he was never coming home.

Sure, sometimes I felt like I'd never be whole again. And sure the times that I didn't feel like that in recent memory were with someone I couldn't currently even send a BeReal to without having a four-minute power cry afterwards.

But I was fine.

What wasn't fine was all of the people I loved most in the

world banding together to keep a secret from me and lying to me for over a year. That shit was fucked up.

I tapped the trackpad of my laptop with way more force than needed, opening my folders and scrolling to find the campaign image I'd been editing. In my frustration I'd scrolled way back into last year. A photo caught my eye immediately, followed by the usual ache in my stomach after I'd imagined seeing Chris.

But it wasn't my imagination. I clicked on the photo, blowing it up from a thumbnail to taking up most of the screen. It was us, taking a selfie on the subway while we headed to see Chris' doctor. I pressed the back directional arrow, watching as Chris appeared to recover as time moved in reverse.

The more I looked at the photos, the more my stomach filled with lead. There was an obvious decline in his health after treatment ... but why had I never noticed how skinny he'd gotten before his diagnosis? Or how tired he looked?

When I looked back at our memories in my mind, I couldn't remember seeing a difference in Chris, which is why his diagnosis caught me so off guard. But looking back at these pictures, I should have noticed *something*.

I paused when I got to our anniversary in August, getting up from where I was on the couch to grab a bottle of gin and a glass. I didn't bother with the tonic water. Seeing how happy we were felt like a punch to the gut.

How the fuck did I miss everything? Was I that horrible of a fiancé that I couldn't even notice that something had been seriously wrong with him?

When I settled back onto my spot on the sofa, my phone was vibrating again. I sighed and picked up, putting it on speaker.

"What, Lexie?" I didn't bother to keep the frustration out of my voice.

Why was it so hard for her to leave me alone to get drunk and wallow in my own self pity?

If I was honest, I'm not even sure who I was mad at now. Of course lying to me was a major dickhead move and the betrayal of it all hurt like a bitch—a white hot knife stabbing me in the back would have been preferable—but the longer I sat with it, the more guilt I felt.

Like somehow maybe *I* was the reason Chris kept the secret from me.

"It's New Year's Eve Eve Hazel, how long are you going to do this?"

"Haven't decided."

My hand clenched the glass bottle, fingers digging into the side of it. I *really* didn't want to talk about this right now. All of the emotions that I had been keeping carefully locked inside threatened to burst the moment her voice filtered through the phone.

"Everyone would really like to see you—even hear from you. I know you're icing them all out."

"The only reason you're not on the do not call list is because of the gift certificate to a very nice masseuse."

She sighed through the receiver.

"And because you don't pry," I finished, using my teeth to uncork the bottle of gin and spitting it out onto my trendy hand woven low pile carpet.

Even living in this house pissed me off.

Especially knowing Chris bought it with me only to find out he was terminal a month later. Infinity especially because when that happened his stupid fucking life insurance covered the whole thing, which left me with no mortgage and a small fortune. Despite the fact that we weren't married yet.

All the things he'd prepared for me before he died became so much more obvious as time went on. Many of the utilities had been paid out months ahead of time. His Amazon account showed purchases for small gifts that had led up to three months after his passing, ones which I couldn't force myself to cancel.

Each reminder was painful and every time I tried to push those feelings away they only multiplied; it wasn't long before they started to decay—leaving me sick to my stomach.

"Hazel, I won't tell you what to do with your life babe—"

"Good," I snapped, sloshing a healthy amount of gin into the glass and setting the bottle on the table. I needed something to calm the emotions, and fast.

"But, the people waiting in that bar love you. I love you. Qui—"

"Don't you dare, Lex."

"No, you need to hear it Haze. In fact, open the fucking door. It's freezing out here."

"I'm not home." I lied wildly. Seeing her would only worsen everything and I wasn't sure if I would be able to hold onto the angry facade if we were face to face.

Then she'd really see it. How much it hurts. How much everything fucking hurts. Because for two days, *two days*, I felt like myself again.

"I can see you through the curtains, asshole. Open up or I'll use my key."

I groaned and pushed myself off the sofa, padding through the living room to the townhouse's front door. The second I'd undone the deadbolt, Lexie was already pushing her way in and slamming the door shut behind her with pink cheeks. Her eyes went immediately to the bottle and glass, then the computer.

I steeled myself by taking a deep breath and counting down from three in my head.

"Please tell me you weren't working." She sighed, not bothering to kick off her boots as she headed for the coffee table, turning the laptop towards her with a wince. "Fuck, tell me you were working."

"I was," I hedged. "Then I thought I'd just..."

"Flog yourself until you drank an entire bottle of gin, all the while knowing that the one person you can actually talk to about this stuff and who gets it is so desperate for your attention that they are about to send a carrier pigeon to your house because you are too stubborn to call her?"

Annoyance pricked my skin.

"Oh, fuck off." I grabbed my glass and took a long drink, throwing myself back down onto the couch. "Lexie, I already told you. All the while she was telling me that she wanted me and that she loved me, she was lying right to my face!"

Lexie kicked her shoes in the general direction of the door and met me on the sofa, bringing the laptop around with her. "I have a hard time believing that Quinn—*the* Quinn—said the words I love you to anyone."

"Well she did," I grumbled, turning my eyes back to the screen. I pressed the backward key, showing yet another photo of Chris, Quinn, and I.

Fuck, I was sick of wanting her. Sick of being mad at her. Sick of feeling sorry that I said that stuff to her.

"Ooh I remember this!" Lexie said, grabbing the bottle off the table and taking a quick swig. "Fashion week last year— Jesus, Chris was skinny."

I sighed, running a hand over my hair. "Yeah, I had to get his pants brought to the tailor twice in three weeks. A few months later and he was gone." I drained my glass, shaking the ice around in front of Lexie's face. She filled my glass back up and I pressed through a few more photos.

"You know," she said thoughtfully, the gin pinking her

cheeks. "I never realized how much the three of you were together."

"Yup," I said noncommittally. I didn't want to talk about either of them, not really, but I also couldn't seem to stop myself from torturing myself with memories of the two people I loved most.

"Hey! Stop!" She poked at the screen, in danger of sloshing drinks all over the both of us. "Ugh, I always loved that jacket." Lexie whined about Chris' primary colored vintage ski jacket. The photo was from the last Christmas we spent together— Alex, Quinn, and Chris grinning beside the sloppiest made snowman I'd ever seen.

They'd used a bottle of fireball as its nose. Assholes.

"It's hideous Lex," I scolded. "Aren't you a designer?"

"Sure, but that doesn't mean I can't appreciate a classic."

"You can have it if you want," I said, pushing myself up and staggering to the half closet to sift through hangers.

"Really?" She hopped up behind me, flicking on the hall light.

As if I needed it. This neon pink and yellow monstrosity practically was its own light source.

I slipped it off the hanger and set it into Lexie's waiting grabby hands.

She threw it on immediately, moaning with appreciation as she tilted her face to the ceiling. "I love you Chris! This jacket is amazing! I'll give it a great new home."

I laughed, closing the closet behind me. "I'm sure he'd be thrilled that someone is giving it some love."

Lexie checked herself out in the mirror attached to the closet door, unzipping the pockets and shoving her hands inside for the full effect of trudging through a snowy New York City.

"What's this?" she said in surprise, pulling a small, folded piece of paper from inside and offering it to me.

I turned it over in my hands. It was addressed to Quinn in Chris' all too familiar sloped handwriting.

Maybe I was drunk. Maybe I was lonely and wanted to see what Chris had thought to say. Maybe I was mad enough at Quinn that I was suddenly cool opening stuff clearly meant for her. Whatever the reason, I unfolded the page, smoothing it flat with my hands.

"What's it say?" Lexie asked curiously, coming behind me to read along.

Q,

I think you and I both know that I've owed you an apology for a long time. Uncool of me to steal your girl when you already called dibs. But, I did end up with cancer, so I guess we're even, right?

When I'm gone, tell her about the promise right away. Blame me for everything so she doesn't hate you for being a good friend to me when I needed it most. She'll be hurt, but I know she'll forgive you. She's always loved you first, whether she realized it or not.

I needed these last few months. To have one person in my life who didn't look at me like I was a dying man. Who treated me as a person. Not a person with cancer. I know she would've wanted to know—fuck I almost told her a couple *times—but then she'd get talking about the wedding, or the next trip she was taking us on or would give me the more burnt grilled cheese and I'd just find myself being grateful. To me, Hazel has been everything.*

My right now. My future. The love of my life, however short it was.

In part, I have you to thank for that—you did give me permission after all.

Love her the way she deserves. The way you've always wanted to. I won't even haunt your ass for it.

– C

I flipped the page over, desperate for just a few more lines. Chris didn't disappoint.

P.S. Okay, maybe I'll haunt you a little. She was supposed to be my wife. Not your ass though, maybe like your kitchen or something.

I clutched the paper in my hand, my throat threatening to close.

He knew. Of course, he knew. I loved Chris. I loved his humor and his charm. The way he held doors open for old ladies and always said please and thank you to servers. The way he hummed while he did the dishes.

But Quinn? We were written in the stars from the second I

saw her at that freshman mixer and we fucked each other's brains out on that pool table in the frat house.

And she loved me enough that she'd do anything—even walk away from me forever—rather than string me along. She wasn't commitment-phobic at all. *She just committed to the wrong things.*

I am such a fucking asshole.

"Holy shit," Lexie muttered. "So Quinn–"

"Yeah," I grabbed my jacket off the hanger and threw it on over my sweatpants.

"Hey! Where are you going—and dressed like *that?*"

"The bar," I said quickly, shoving the paper into my pocket and grabbing my keys. "Hurry your ass up. I need to get there before she leaves."

Lexie's face split into a grin. "Are you going to—"

"Yes, put your fucking shoes on. The love of my life is waiting for me at a shitty dive bar thinking I hate her." I shoved my feet into my boots and dashed onto the snowy street to wave down a taxi.

Wait for me Quinn, I have something I need to say to you.

Chapter 14
Quinn

"You should've just kept your mouth shut," Alex mumbled as he maneuvered onto his bar stool.

I didn't miss the way his front brushed past Matt's. Or how he plopped into his seat as soon as he realized I was watching.

Matt was sitting with his arm behind his chair, causing him to face Alex. When he noticed Alex's behavior, he straightened and turned towards me with a forced smile.

The bar was busy with patrons, odd for a New Year's Eve Eve. Their voices filled the room, but it wasn't enough to drown the last words Hazel said to me.

You're the worst of them.

The words had been playing in my mind on repeat since she'd left like some twisted up Christmas carol.

The worst part was that I couldn't even dispute it—she'd all but confirmed my fears, things I'd already know about myself—and that made it so *easy* to fall further and further into the darkness with no way out.

But I deserved every single word, no matter how much it hurt.

This was *my* punishment for keeping a secret I damn well knew wasn't supposed to be kept in the first place.

I'd grown close to Chris, especially in the months between getting his diagnosis and telling Hazel. I was the first person he told, and the first one he mourned with. The one who talked him through the reality of his situation. In the moment, while he clung to my shirt and begged me not to say anything—I thought that I was making the right choice.

But just like me, Chris had his own selfish streak. It's not that he didn't want Hazel to know because it hurt *her*... It was because he wanted a few more months to pretend like he wasn't dying.

And who could blame him?

All I wanted was to lie on my couch and drink all the painful thoughts away. It was the only thing that dulled any of the pain ... but my friends would not have it.

Maybe it's because they recognized the beginnings of my spiral and were desperately trying to pull me out of it before I became just like Hazel.

A living ghost.

So here I was, letting them drag me out of the house only for them to lecture me—*again*—on what happened back at the cabin.

"She deserved to know," I grumbled, clutching my drink in my fist. Nausea swirled in my stomach.

I hate how it tore us apart but after seeing how much it hurt her, I was more upset with myself for keeping it from her than telling her. Telling her had been a mercy on us all.

Chris' secret had shackled us with guilt and as much as I didn't want to blame the dead,I couldn't help the sour taste spreading across my tastebuds whenever I thought of him.

How had they lived with themselves?

Maybe it just boiled down how close each of us were to her. As much as I tried to push her away and deny myself, my feelings for her never wavered. Even after a year of no contact, Hazel was the only person I'd be able to call my best friend.

"That Chris was slowly dying and she could do nothing about it?" Alex grumbled under his breath.

"That her friends chose a dead man's dignity over her," I spat back.

Alex's body puffed and Matt scrambled to defuse the tension between us.

"Hey, *hey*, it's the holidays guys, we're supposed to be enjoying our time together." He leaned forward and clasped his hand on my wrist. It wasn't quite pity, wasn't quite kindness in his eyes as he looked me over. I hated every moment of it. "He's being a grump because he feels just as bad as you do. If anything, tonight is for all of us."

I threw back the rest of the whiskey in my glass, wiping the excess from the corner of my mouth.

I hadn't been here long, but this was already my third drink. Them bringing me out did nothing for my routine. If anything, it was just a change of scenery. I would still be getting drunk off my ass at home.

When I didn't respond, Matt squeezed my wrist.

"Have you tried to talk to her?" he asked. "Max and Lexie will be here soon, but it would be nice to have Hazel as well. Maybe give her a call?"

I narrowed my eyes at him.

"You think I haven't tried?"

I had tried every way I knew of to get in contact with her. Call. Text. Instagram. Snapchat. BeReal. Facebook. Discord. Twitter. Fuck I even emailed her.

But she left me in the dark.

Just like I did her.

The alcohol was pushing me to whip out my phone and try again right then and there.

As much as I was fucking killing myself over this whole thing, I wanted nothing more than to hear her voice again. Even if it was to cuss me out some more. Anything would be better than this.

Countless times I'd scrolled through her page, trying to find every video I could in hope to hear her. Every night I dreamed of her—like movies of memories from the cabin and back in college.

I'm a fucking mess.

"Maybe go to her house?" Alex said, interrupting my spiraling thoughts.

I wanted to so bad. The need to go see here *right then* was overwhelming.

I blamed it on the alcohol.

The folded up drawing burned in my pocket. It was the only thing that could keep my attention recently. Client work be damned.

It'd started a simple drawing back in the cabin when Hazel and I were snowed in. It was of her, in the snow, laughing. It was right after she hit me with a snowball and the image of her was burned into my mind because it had been so long since I had seen her so happy. So unburdened.

I brought it on a whim.

I didn't think she would show up, not truly. But for some reason the thought of leaving it alone, in my dark apartment, was heartbreaking.

I waved the bartender over for another drink. Matt and Alex had realized quickly after that I wasn't in the mood for talking but his words swirled in my head.

She wasn't answering and knowing Hazel, she was probably not much better off than me. If anything, she had been forced back into her grief and I *really* didn't want to think of what that would look like for her.

I stood abruptly, Matt and Alex's eyes following my movements.

"I'll pay you back," I murmured and grabbed my coat before turning towards the exit.

Matt gasped, a triumphant look on his face as he waved his phone at me. "Wait! Lexie is on her way and she's with—"

His voice was cut off as I pushed out of the bar and into the cold night.

I was much drunker by the time I made it to Hazel's brownstone. I'd accidentally given the Uber an address a block over, so drunk Quinn had to march through the cold, snow covered streets, in order to find her place.

The city was alive even at that late hour before the holiday. Taxis and cars were winding through the streets honking at each other. People singing and shouting. It was the sounds of the city that sobered me enough to complete the trip.

My knees were wobbly and by the time I got to her door. I had no energy to knock. Instead I slumped down with my back against the wall and dug the paper out from my pocket.

I let out a sigh as I looked at it.

It wasn't my best work, and still very much a sketch, but her expression was captured perfectly. I traced the side of her face with my finger that was quickly becoming numb from the cold.

She still has my gloves, I thought with a bitter tone.

"I'm sorry," I said, not at all trying to lower my voice. I knew she probably wouldn't hear me. Maybe she would even be asleep ... but I still needed to say it.

"I never wanted to hurt you," I said, dragging myself back to my feet. I leaned my forehead against the door, imagining her just beyond it, leaning with her ear against the door in hopes to hear what I was saying.

Hoping that she had missed me as much as I missed her.

"I fucked up, I know ... but I really thought I was doing what was best for you. Because..." I let out a sigh and ran my hand through my hair. "I love you. I always have and I wanted you to have a chance at happiness. I *never* wanted to take that from you."

I waited for a few minutes, listening for any possible signs of life behind the door ... but all I could hear was my own heartbeat.

It was stupid to come to her door like this. *Pathetic.* She deserved more than this. More than what I could give her.

I had been so lost in loving then avoiding her then loving her again to stop and think that maybe it was *me* who was the problem. Maybe none of this worked out because I was not enough.

And showing up to her house late at night on December 30th with a shitty drawing wasn't going to be what would prove to her that you were sorry, or that you truly did love her as much as you said.

I slipped the drawing through the mail slot and turned, it took me a while to get down the short flight of stairs. Like all the whiskey was really starting to catch up to me. It was even longer to get back to my apartment, but the cold was what helped me formulate a plan to *really* get her back.

I wouldn't half ass this any more.

I wanted—*needed*—her back and there was only one way worthy of grabbing her attention.

Chapter 15

Quinn

"I'm *so* getting fired for this," Eric muttered under his breath from his place at my side.

I turned to him with a nervous smile spreading across my face, our bodies crushed together from the excited crowd filling Times Square.

New Year's Eve.

I hated how many people were brushing up against me.

How loud they talked.

Matt, Alex, and Max were somewhere in the crowd to my right and Lexie was on the other side of Eric, their fingers loosely intertwined.

"You think she'll show?" I asked, running a hand over my hair, I'd ditched my perfunctory beanie for the occasion.

Lexie bit her lip and looked away. A wistful, faraway expression on her face. "No idea."

The group of us had been waiting for hours, staring up at one of the biggest flashing billboards in the square, waiting for our queue.

Everything was set, now we just had to wait.

For Hazel.

I'd left her so many voicemails that I'd filled her inbox—sure half of them were the garbled, drunken nonsense of four a.m. planning this crazy apology Quinn, but some of them were really heartfelt. The only sign that she was even thinking of me was the read receipts on Instagram—those messages she was definitely looking at.

I had skipped past begging and went straight to groveling. That if there was *any* part of her that loved me, hell, or even just loved our friends, that she would show up tonight.

It was a gamble ... but I prayed it would work out. It had to. And not just because Eric was looking greener by the second, sweat beading at his temples nervously.

A billboard in Times Square on New Year's Eve? Yeah, he was so getting fucking fired.

My breath caught when the timer on the billboard started counting down from five minutes.

"I don't know how, but I'll find you a job," I promised, gripping my phone so hard in my pocket the screen was liable to snap in half.

"Just invite me to the wedding," he countered, slinging his arm around Lexie's shoulders.

Lexie snorted with laughter that she attempted to poorly disguise with a cough.

"That's what it's for right?" he asked. "At the end of this? Don't tell me your only motive is to get her to forgive you!"

I swallowed thickly as my face began to heat—clearing my throat as I looked out at the crowd. Four minutes to go as still no sign of her.

Maybe she really wouldn't come.

"Forgiveness would be a good start," I said, rubbing my hand along the back of my neck. "But a girl can dream, can't she?"

He nudged my side with a light laugh.

I pulled out my phone—my heart catching in my throat as I saw there were still no messages from Hazel. Before I could overthink it I unlocked the device and dialed her number from memory, bringing the receiver to my ear.

Each ring caused my body to tense.

Ring, ring, ring.

Was she really not going to show?

Ring, ring. Ring.

Could she really fall out of love with me that quickly?

On the seventh ring, she picked up.

I heard the voices of the crowd first, followed by a string of curses that would make even a sailor blush.

"Where are you guys?" she yelled. "It's so packed I can't get through!—Ugh—Get out of my way!"

I was so stunned that I couldn't speak. My heart was pounding in my chest like I'd run a marathon.

She's here. She's here!

"Quinn?" she asked. "Quinn, can you hear me? Damn this crowd."

"You're here," I breathed. By some miracle, she heard me.

"Like I would miss New Year's Eve in Times Square? Listen, Quinn I don't want to go into next year without saying this, and the over phone is totally not how I wanted this to go —" she scoffed.

I laughed and waved my phone in the air.

Lexie leaned into Eric, her lips practically against his ear as she whispered to him. Matt pushed through the ground of people separating us, Max's hand clutched in his hand like she was a bridge between him and Alex. The grouchy tech mogul looked at me sidelong, his glasses fogged from his breath and the cold air.

"She's here!" I yelled while covering the receiver.

Matt's smile was blinding. He pulled Alex and Max close, the taller, broodier of the two pushing him away with a scowl.

I pretended not to notice, whipping around to grin at Eric as he squeezed my shoulder.

"Hurry," he yelled over the crowd. The numbers were counting down steadily on the screen, the excitement in the air rising to a tangible thing as we got closer to the ball drop. I caught sight of the billboard, it was playing a clothing ad for a luxury retailer with way too much money—and was our warning to get ready.

"Where are you?" I yelled into the phone. "What do you see?"

"A wall of people!" she yelled. "I'm close to the Express ad!"

I searched the square for the ad and cringed when I realized how far away it was. She would just be able to see the screen, but it would be a stretch to reach her in time.

"Walk towards One Times Square," I ordered. "I can meet you in the middle!"

I pushed through the crowd with way too much force, but I didn't care about their curses or anger. All I cared about was getting to Hazel.

She came!

"I can't move much!" she yelled.

I cursed and looked back towards the billboard. The ad was starting.

"Look up!" I yelled. "Look towards the bright yellow screen with black writing!"

"What? Quinn look I can't—"

"Please," I begged. "*Please* look up at the damn screen Haze."

I moved through the crowd. She gasped quietly.

I knew what she was seeing. I'd spent all night gathering all the pictures of her and I that I could find. I originally thought to add our friends as well, to remind her how much we loved her ... but like Eric said, I had other motives.

Entirely selfish ones at that.

Chris wasn't wrong when he said that Hazel could've been the girl he married. But what he got wrong is that Hazel *is* the girl that I marry. No matter how long it takes.

"Quinn— how did you—"

"I'm sorry Haze," I said, looking around the crowd, hoping to find those familiar green eyes staring back at me. "I am so sorry. I cannot even describe how much it killed me to see you hurt. All I wanted—"

"Quinn," she breathed. "Where are you?"

"Please just let me finish," I said.

I peered back at the ad to see it still showing our pictures. "All I wanted was to see you happy, but because of that I made selfish decisions. Ones that ended up hurting you far more than I ever realized. So please, come back to us. To me. I promise to make this up to you."

I love you in fancy cursive lit up the screen, but I was met with silence on the other line.

People started chanting all around us.

"10!"

"9!"

"Where are you?" she yelled finally.

With a heavy heart, I looked up to the ball.

"I do love you Haze," I whispered. "There never anyone else for me. *Never.*"

"3!"

"2!"

The cries were deafening. Time slowed. I looked around for Hazel one more time, but I realized it was useless.

"1!"

I was jerked forward by a hand grabbing my jacket and pulling me down. Hazel's bright green eyes and wicked smile filled my vision. Her cheeks were flushed and she was breathing heavily. Before the relief of seeing her could crash through me voices rang out around us.

"Happy New Year!"

Chapter 16

Hazel

Way Too Early That Morning

Quinnlan Strouse was a beautiful idiot.

Last night I showed up to the bar to find out that she'd drank herself stupid and then fucked off right before I arrived, so I went to her place. I waited for 45 minutes in the freezing cold in the most breezy pair of sweatpants to exist for her not to bother showing up.

And when I went to call her to chew her out for not being here, to ask her who she was with and what the fuck she thought she was doing ruining my big romantic gesture—my phone was dead.

Typical.

By the time I got back to my apartment I was pre-hypothermic, pissed off, and a little hungover.

Then, I saw the drawing.

Beautiful. Smart. Compassionate. Loyal. *Idiot.*

She'd come back to my apartment instead of her own, we'd likely just missed each other. It was always like that for Quinn and I. Just two ships passing on the water without ever really colliding.

I was sick of it.

The next time I saw that woman it would be with a fucking plan. Which meant that I did what any reasonable, self-sufficient woman in New York City would—I got my ass up at the crack of dawn, took the subway to the Upper East Side, grabbed an egregiously priced bagel and waited for Tiffany's to open.

I leaned against the shop's facade, irritation burning through me. Quinn had been blowing up my phone all fucking morning, asking if I was going to come to the square like we did every year as if I wanted the first time I told her that I loved her —that she actually heard—to be over Instagram.

Not a chance.

I took an irritated bite out of my bagel as my phone started to vibrate in my pocket again.

With a quick glance, I opened up the messages between Quinn and I.

Apology after apology and then finally—

QUINNTATTS

Please just meet me tonight, I'm begging you.
Even if it's only to kick my ass. Please come.

Finally, the door to the shop unlocked and I ditched my bagel in a nearby trashcan before hurrying inside.

Oh, I'd be meeting her alright. She could count on it.

The day did *not* go as I planned.

I'd left the shop with a small bag and big dreams—only to have them crushed when I got an email from one of my biggest clients, letting me know that the video proof I'd sent over for a campaign that needed to be approved by *midnight* had been corrupted. It'd taken me sixteen hours of post production the first time I'd completed the ad reel and I had less than 12 hours by the time I got to my flat to do it again.

So, I *crunched.*

By 11:15p.m. I had the file exporting onto the shared company drive and I was pulling on my jacket to leave.

The second the little '*successful transfer*' message popped up, I was out the door and bolting for the subway. It would be impossible to take a taxi anywhere near Times Square right now, and I needed to be in the center of it within 45 minutes.

I popped out of the subway a few blocks from where I wanted to be, my hand closing around the little aquamarine blue box in my pocket like a lifeline as I sprinted, narrowly dodging partygoers on my way towards the ball.

The minutes were ticking down and my progress had all but stalled out as I was met with a crowd so tightly packed that not even years of mosh pit experience would get me through.

My phone began to ring in my pocket and I let out a frustrated huff, expecting to see Lexie's name on the screen—surprise and nerves skittered through me as Quinn's contact flashed.

"Quinn? Quinn, can you hear me? Damn this crowd!" I grunted with frustration as I tried to wedge myself between groups of people, fighting to get to our usual spot.

"You're here," Quinn breathed, little more than a whisper.

"Like I would miss New Year's Eve in Times Square," I teased. This wasn't how this was supposed to go, but there was no way I was going to get through in time. The minute countdown had already started. "Listen, Quinn I don't want to go into next year without saying this, and the phone is totally not how I wanted this to go but I am so sorry, I never should have said that shit. We were both just doing our best."

Quinn's muffled voice came through the receiver, there was too much static for me to make out what she was saying.

"Quinn? Can you hear me?" I shouted, frustration burning through me.

Stupid ad! I was supposed to be *early*!

"Where are you?" Quinn yelled through the speaker. "What do you see?"

I let out a bitter laugh. "A wall of people! I'm close to the Express ad!"

"Walk towards One Times Square," she ordered, bossy as ever. "I can meet you in the middle."

I was almost totally surrounded, and with my height it was impossible to see much of where I was going.

"I can't move much!"

Quinn cursed. "Look up! Look towards the bright yellow screen with black writing!"

"What?" I asked, bewildered. "Quinn look I can't—"

"Please," She begged. "*Please,* look up at the damn screen Haze."

I turned my eyes towards the screen—barely able to see over the heads of the people around me—and gasped.

Photos. Dozens of beautifully curated images from the best moments of my entire life lit Times Square.

"Quinn—" I breathed, my heart hammering against my chest. I thought I was going to be the one with the big romantic gesture. Leave it to Quinn to steal that too. "How did you—"

"I'm sorry Haze. I am so sorry. I cannot even describe to you how much it killed me to see you hurt. All I wanted—"

"Quinn," I breathed. "Where are you?"

We couldn't do this over the phone. I needed to see her. Right now.

"Please just let me finish," she pleaded, but I didn't hear anything else. I kept my eyes on the screen as best as I could, pushing through the crowd with renewed enthusiasm.

The screen lit with the words I'd been dying to tell her since the second I saw her again at the cabin and I broke, tears splashing down my cheeks as people started chanting all around us.

"10!"

No, I wouldn't go into the New Year without her.

"9!"

"Where are you?" I yelled into the phone.

"I do love you Haze," she whispered her voice coming in double, I was *close*. "There was never anyone else for me. *Never*."

"3!"

I caught sight of a ruffle of messy, curly, dirty blonde hair.

"2!"

"Get out of the fucking way!" I shouted and the final barrier between us fell away, I reached forward, my fingers closing around the front of Quinn's jacket.

"1!"

Her beautiful aquamarine eyes met mine and, for a second that felt like a hundred years, we gaped at each other, a smile tugging at the corners of my mouth. Her flushed face, the hickeys I'd left a little over a week ago that'd faded to almost nothing on the side of her neck. The dimples of her cheeks, surprised into revealing themselves just for me.

"Happy New Year!"

I pulled her down to my level, crushing my lips against her in a desperate, gasping kiss.

"Quinn—"

"Haze—"

"No shut up," I demanded. "I love you. I'm so sorry, I shouldn't have freaked out like that. It wasn't fair."

"Wait—"

"No!" I gripped the front of her shirt, eyes streaming. "I have loved you since the second I laid eyes on you Quinn, you incredibly tall, gorgeous, intelligent, kind *idiot!*"

"But—"

"For once in your life, can you listen to me! I've never met anyone who talks so little who loves the sound of her own voice as much as—" My tirade was cut off as her lips met mine for a feverish, sucking kiss, Quinn's arms banding around me as she laughed.

"Marry me," she crooned in my ear, stepping back to pull a small box out of her pocket.

"That's my fucking line!" I shouted, pulling out the blue box and waving it in front of her face. "If you could just li—"

Quinn howled with delirious laughter, pressing kisses everywhere she could reach. "You impossible woman, marry me!"

I groaned and sagged into her, gripping her face the best I could with the small box in my hand and kissing her hard. "Yes, you idiot. A million, trillion times, yes."

Quinn

My skin itched as I shifted in the far too constricting suit.

My palms were sweaty and my heart had been nonstop pounding in my chest since the moment I had taken my place.

The sun was shining bright overhead and a light breeze passed through the area, cooling my heated skin. It was a perfect fall day at Stargazer's Lake. The air was chilly, but not enough where we needed to bundle up. The trees had started to run various shades of red, orange, and yellow, and looked like they had come straight out of a painting.

We had taken over an area near the north of the lake that was often used for concerts and other events. Usually, it fit a few hundred people at a time, but the group of family and close friends was enough for us.

White chairs were lined in front of me with a braided rope of flowers on either side of them, making a short, but perfect aisle. Trees surrounded the space and Hazel had taken extra care to place wrap vines of white roses around the trees.

People were already in their seats and chatting excitedly. Light music was weaving through the area and mixing with the voices. Many were taking pictures of me, my groomsmen, and the beautiful lake behind me.

In just a few moments the sun would set and provide the perfect backdrop for the ceremony. Cameras were propped up at every edge, constantly running in order to get every perfect moment. We had had a few of our friends, as well as a hired videographer and photographer ready to capture the moment that had been both the height of my life and the source of all my anxiety through the last few months.

All eyes were on me.

My skin crawled with attention and I couldn't help but wish that we had made this whole thing that much smaller.

But Hazel would love it. And that's what was important.

We had taken extra steps to make sure that this place was picture-perfect. After all, Hazel would need it for social media. She had gotten an influx of sponsorships as soon as she announced her wedding. Hell, they had paid for most of the wedding expenses.

I turned to look at the people behind me. Both Matt and Alex had been more than willing to stand up here with me, something that meant more to me than I could ever verbalize to either of them. It was not just their support, but acceptance of Hazel and I. They were our friends and had pushed us together jokingly, but actions spoke louder than words.

There was one more thing that made my heart clench...

My eyes dropped to the chair right behind me. It was the same one the guests were sitting in but decked out in the same flowers that lined the aisle and trees. And right in the middle ... was a picture of Chris.

It was one that Hazel had taken when they were at Stargazer's Lake and one of the last ones taken before his diagnosis. He was happy and so full of life that it almost felt like he really was here with us.

He had asked me once, before he proposed to Hazel, if I would do the honor of being his best man. I laughed it off stating that he should get an *actual* man, but he insisted it be me. His ask had gutted me while simultaneously making me feel like the most important person in the world.

What I never got to tell him was that if the roles were reversed, I would have had him standing behind me in a heartbeat. There was no one I would've rather had.

But at the time, I never thought this day would ever come. I thought instead that it would be Chris in my place. Something I would have regretted for the rest of my life.

I looked ahead of me and met Max's gaze. She was wearing a long orangish flowy gown, a part of the palette that Lexie had chosen for the ceremony. It complimented her skin and hair perfectly. She gave me a tense smile and pulled a tissue out from her bra before dabbing her eyes.

It was enough to crack the tenseness in my body.

Lexie leaned to the side from behind her and gave me a smile. She wore a similar gown as Max, though hers was in a warm taupe color. Hazel and I had no problem giving her full control over the colors of the wedding given that she had a knack for it.

She had painstakingly sewed both hers and Max's dresses and helped those who were wearing suits tailor them.

The shift in the music caused me to stand straight and look down the aisle. My hair stood up on the back of my neck and my heart skipped a beat in my chest.

It was almost time.

Max's niece, Madelyn, was the first one down the aisle. She had on a puffy white dress that threatened to swallow her and held a basket of white rose petals in her hand. She was a ball of joy and had been so excited when she was asked to be our flower girl. People let out gasps of delight and chuckled when the wrinkled face of Milo strutted down the aisle after the girl.

Madelyn was but seven years old and let out an excited giggle when Milo reached her. He was not very well-behaved but everyone, including our flower girl, seemed to enjoy the light interruption. She paused to reach down and give him a loving pat on the head before continuing with her duty.

When she reached the end of the aisle she gave me a beaming smile, one I returned wholeheartedly. She turned toward Max who beckoned her to come over. Milo tried to follow her but I was quick to grab for him.

With a barely contained sigh, I stood up and held him in my arms. Contrary to what I portrayed to the group, it was an easy decision to adopt him after the trip. In the last year, he had grown to his full size, though luckily he stayed small enough for us to carry him.

I quickly untied the rings from the back of his collar before holding him tight to my side. People let out cued 'aws' when he licked my face.

My breath was stolen when I caught sight of Hazel.

She's beautiful.

She always had been, but seeing her in her wedding dress was something of a fantasy of mine. She chose a dress with flutter sleeves, a deep plunging neckline that cinched at the waist and then puffed out delicately right above her hips, topped with a layer of delicate lace over the entire thing.

It fit her and the lake perfectly.

Most of her hair was falling in waves down her back save for a few pieces that were pinned back, showing off her flushed face. She had a smile on her face and her eyes nervously drifted across the guests before they landed on me.

My throat tightened and tears pricked my eyes.

Shit, don't cry.

Matt was by my side at a moment's notice, taking Milo from me. I tried to shoot him a grateful smile, but couldn't pull my eyes from Hazel. Her father, Mitch, was at her side leading her down the aisle, but he was far from my mind.

I had never felt as ready for something than I did in that moment. Without having to be prompted, I took her hand from Mitch's. I couldn't even manage to send him a smile because of how enamored I was by Hazel.

It's finally happening. I can't believe this is happening.

After everything, I was finally going to be able to call her my wife. I knew, realistically, that nothing would change between us because of the title, but *goddamn* would it feel good to say.

"You look beautiful," I whispered.

"You don't look too bad yourself," she teased, a smile spreading across her face.

I was ready to grab her and kiss her right then and there. I had trouble listening to the officiant as he went through the ceremony because it took so much for me to hold back.

I was at a loss for words. The whole thing didn't even feel real.

"Quinn and Hazel have both written vows," the officiant said, interrupting my trance. "Quinn may start."

I cleared my throat and stood up straight. I know people probably expected me to bring out a paper, but I had long since decided that I wouldn't need it because I would be speaking the words that had run rampant in my head for years.

"Hazel, you're the person I had been waiting for since the moment I took my first breath," I said through the knot in my throat. "You are my best friend, the love of my life, and the only person that I want to be with for the rest of our days. It may have taken me a while to understand what I was feeling for you." Alex muttered something under his breath and I heard his sharp intake of breath from what I guessed was Matt giving him a sharp nudge. I let out a small chuckle. "It did. Truly took me far too long, I was scared. I thought that I didn't deserve someone as perfect and loving as you. That there would be someone better suited." We all knew who. "But I have always loved you and I promise from here on out to love you every day like it was our last so that there is no more time wasted between us. I promise to take care of you when you're sick, and let you put your cold feet on my stomach even though you know how much I hate it."

There were laughs throughout the crowd.

Hazel's eyes glistened and she blinked rapidly to stop the tears from flowing.

"I promise not to get caught up in our petty arguments and to learn and grow with you so that we may never grow bored, just learn new ways to love each other" I took a deep breath. "There is nothing more than I could ask from this world. I love you Hazel and ever since you stepped into my life I knew that there was no turning back. I can't wait to spend the rest of our lives together and am excited to see what else lies ahead because I know that with you by my side, every moment will be more than anything I could have ever wished for."

The officiant nodded for Hazel to start and she sniffed loudly, offering a watery smile.

"Fuck, I didn't think we'd ever get to do this." She dropped my hand and took a handkerchief from Lexie, using it to dab at her streaming eyes. "Gimme a sec."

Giggles and murmurs followed as she took a deep breath, handing the handkerchief back to Lexie and putting a hand over her heart.

"I've been so fortunate to find someone I love in this life, not just once but twice—and I know Chris is up there with the smuggest, most annoying smile on his face thinking that he's the one who finally pushed us together. He's wrong though. From the moment I first saw you, Quinn, and that stupid faux-hawk haircut you used to have—"

Matt whooped beside us and I breathed a laugh.

"I knew that our story was going to end in one of two ways. With me heartbroken, wishing I'd never met you " She smiled wryly, grabbing my hands and giving them a light squeeze. "Or right here, swearing to you that I'm going to love you forever—more than mini marshmallows or the first big rain of spring. Even more than a mall pretzel, so you know it's serious."

Laughs and sniffles erupted from the group.

"I've spent my entire adult life traveling the globe, searching for something that made me feel the way I did when I looked into your eyes for the first time. But none of it could ever compare to the feeling that I have right now. You're my home Quinn and I'm going to love your annoying, pig-headed, stupidly kind ass until you're old and all your tattoos look like a weird toddler drew all over you. Until my hair is gray and—well I mean obviously I'm always going to be very sexy—"

I snorted and she swatted at me playfully, tilting her head to the side.

"It'll be me and you until my last breath, Quinn. Forever. It's going to be you and me."

She looked at the officiant, an adorable irritated pout to her lower lip. "Can you just pronounce us already so I can kiss my wife?"

My heart juddered against my chest as the words, the tears I'd been clinging to finally slid free.

"Do you, Quinnlan—"

"Yes," I interrupted.

"And you, Haz—"

"Yes, yes, yes, yes! A million trillion times yes!"

He chuckled good-naturedly, clearly unsure what to do with us, but as Hazel wrapped her arms around my neck, happy tears streaming down her perfectly painted cheeks, I couldn't find it in myself to care.

"You may now—"

"Kiss me, already!" Hazel demanded.

I placed my hands on either side of her face and crashed my lips to hers. I didn't care for the cheers and applause, or that the clicks of the cameras had threatened to drown it all out. All I cared about was the need to be close to her.

I kissed her like it was the last time. I kissed her like it was a lifeline. And most importantly, I kissed her like this kiss alone could put into words just how much I loved her ... because I had no words left to explain just how much she meant to me.

We pulled away breathlessly with people still clapping and cheering around us.

"Put the goddamn rings on already!" Matt yelled from behind us.

We both chuckled, but made no move to do so. The rings were a status symbol for everyone else. Hazel and I both knew that no matter what, we were it for each other.

"I didn't know you could be so sweet," she said with a laugh. "Maybe we will need to redo our vows every year if this is what awaits me."

I gave her one last chaste kiss.

"I'll marry you every year for the rest of our lives if that's what you want," I whispered.

She playfully pushed me away so that she could turn to the crowd with her flowers lifted in the air.

I laughed at her antics and let her pull me down the aisle, excited to step into the rest of our lives together.

❄

"Shh, if you're any louder they'll hear you," I whispered in Hazel's ear as she clenched around my fingers. "If you can't keep quiet, I may be forced to do it myself."

Her groan told me she was open to the idea.

Her wedding dress was bunched up around her waist. I had one hand holding up her leg while the other was buried in between her thighs. Her arms were wrapped around my shoulders and her hands were pulling at my hair. My hair would be a mess after this, but I'm sure Hazel's wouldn't be much better.

She had long since ditched her veil and more than once I had tangled my hands into the silky locks. I couldn't get enough of her.

When I pulled away to get a good look at her face, I noticed that her lipstick was smudged as well. For some reason it only made the need for her grow inside me. She had looked so perfect, so put together, yet I took immense pleasure in ruining it.

I gave her a burning kiss on her lips before trailing kisses down her neck. I pushed her harder against the wall and paused to listen for voices. When there were none, I gave her a light bite on her neck and ground my heel into her clit.

Her gasp sent me spiraling.

The reception was being held at the cabin Chris' parents owned and while I would have very much have liked to mingle with the crowd, I couldn't keep my hands off my wife.

My wife.

The term sounded so sweet in my mind and even better when said aloud. Since the moment I saw her at the end of the aisle, I had the image of seeing her half dressed and begging for me to let her come in my mind.

Hazel had always been beautiful, but there was something about seeing her in a wedding dress that caused me to lose my damn mind.

People were mostly outside enjoying the food and dancing, but there were a few that wandered into the house to get away from all the noise or use the bathroom as needed, threatening to get us caught. And I couldn't let this get cut short.

I curled my fingers inside of her and rubbed circles on her clit with my thumb. She was terrible at keeping quiet but after a while, I began to not care.

So what if they heard us? It's not like we would be stopping anytime soon. And it was our wedding anyways, we deserved a bit of time to ourselves.

Not when she was clutching my suit and begging me not to stop, and not when she came with a cry on my hand. She was so beautiful, and I still couldn't wrap my mind around the fact that she was mine now.

Everything was such a dream come true.

"I love you," I whispered against her lips. "I love you so much."

"I love you too." She shifted and hastily began undoing my pants just enough so she could slip her hand into my underwear.

I let out a low moan as her fingers ran through my already wet folds.

"Admit it," she teased. "You have a thing for wedding dresses."

I buried my head in the crook of her neck as she circled my clit.

"I have a thing for *you* in a wedding dress," I mumbled and bit down lightly on the sensitive skin of her neck.

It was true through, all I could think about as soon as I saw her was how fast I would be able to get the dress around her waist so I could fuck her properly. There was something so erotic about making her come in a dress that had been associated with purity. I wanted to see her makeup smudged and her hair ruined, but I kept that need locked down for later.

I bucked my hips against her when she inserted two fingers inside of me. The pants were restricting our movements and irritated me, but the need to come made everything else fall away.

"God, you're so wet," she moaned.

It was almost embarrassing how obscenely wet I was. I had been fantasizing about this moment for hours, and I knew that in moments I would be coming.

"I can't help it," I murmured into her. My hand was back cupping her pussy before I could stop myself. The feeling of her swollen folds caused a burst of heat to go through me.

She gasped when I pinched her clit.

"One more," I said with a moan. Her motions had quickened and a low heat started to gather in my belly. This time I pushed three fingers into her. She was already clenching around me.

"If we keep going we won't leave here," she said with a light giggle.

I let out a far too loud groan as I came around her fingers. I paused in my ministrations as my orgasm racked my body.

We didn't leave for another fifteen minutes, but by the time we were done and slipped back into the party, it was like no one had noticed that we were gone. People were mingling and laughing as we reentered, all of them totally in their own world and enjoying themselves.

Hazel and I shared conspiratorial smirks as we made our way to the bar and got yet another glass of champagne. I never liked crowds, but there was something so fulfilling about celebrating the love Hazel and I had for each other.

I pulled her to me with a smile.

"Are you happy Mrs. Strouse?" I asked her and leaned down to brush my lips across hers.

"Is that even a question?" She asked with a giggle. "Not only did we have a beautiful ceremony and I get to call you *wife* now but the way you ravish—"

A clearing of a throat caused Hazel and I to break away. My heart dropped when I met the gaze of Chris' parents. His dad, Bob, looked so much like him that it caused my heart to hurt. His mom, Joanne, looked over us with teary eyes and a smile.

"Congrats you two," she said, her voice cracking.

Her husband pulled her into a side hug and sent us a smile.

"We can't tell you how happy we are for you two," he said. "I know Chris would be too."

"Thank you," Hazel said with a small smile.

"It was touching to see him a part of the ceremony," his mom said.

"I couldn't imagine it any other way," I admitted.

She sniffled and nodded. Her husband took it as his queue to dig into his pocket and hold a small black velvet bag out to us. Hazel hesitantly took it from him.

"I wanted to get you before it's too late," he said and turned to look back at the cabin that held so many memories for us all. "As soon as we heard, we knew the perfect gift."

Hazel dug through the bag and pulled out a small house key. It was familiar, but the understanding of it didn't dawn on me until Hazel let out a choked gasp.

"It's too much," she whispered. "We wouldn't dare—"

"It was Chris'," he said, cutting her off. "Or it would have been. A gift from his parents to him, and I couldn't think of anything else I'd want to give you more."

"Believe it or not Hazel," his mom said and stepped forward to grab Hazel. "We still think of you as a part of our family. A daughter, even. So just let us give this gift to you, hm?"

I wrapped my arm around my wife as tears fell down her cheeks.

"Thank you," I said to them. "We will never be able to repay your kindness."

They both smiled at me. Bob walked over and wrapped his arms around his wife as she became teary-eyed.

"Just love each other," he said. "Grow old together. Make each other happy. That will be payment enough."

Hazel leaned into my side, sobbing lightly.

"We will," I promised and leaned down to kiss the top of Hazel's head.

Even without the gift, there was no other type of life waiting for us. I had waited long enough, and from then on out, I would never take even a second of our love together for granted.

And this was only the beginning.

If you liked this, please review!

Reviews really help indie authors so if you likes this book please review on Goodreads and Amazon! More reviews mean more people can see our books and if they do that... then we can write more!

Acknowledgments

Thank you to everyone supporting this book! This is our first book together and without the support from our previous readers there was no way this would be possible!

About Eden Emory

Elle (Eden Emory) is a California native who has lived in Los Angeles for most of her life. From the very start she has been in love with all things fantasy and reading. As soon as Elle found out that writing books was someone's career, she started writing stories. While the first ones were about scorned love and missed opportunities of lunchtime love, she has grown to love all things spicy and paranormal!

For more books like this visit ellemaebooks.com.

For updates on my release schedule and behind the scenes look follow my Instagram @ellemaebooks

Sign-up to my newsletter here https://view.flodesk.com/pages/615e296bf88d548e68f5c7bc for a free short!

For free shorts and NSFW art check out my Patreon! https://www.patreon.com/ellemaebooks

About Bex

Bex (Ashley Pines) is a cat-mom of two, wife and spicy romance enthusiast living in Edmonton, AB. You can usually find her curled up on the sofa surrounded by a hundred pillows and reading on her kindle (or, y'know, writing.) Becoming her best friend is easy! You just need an undying love of all things sweet and be cool with watching the same five movies on repeat.

www.ingramcontent.com/pod-product-compliance
Lightning Source LLC
Chambersburg PA
CBHW060351180626
46817CB00008B/2969